GRANDPA'S HORSE
& OTHER TALES

GRANDPA'S
HORSE

& Other ~~Tails~~ *Tales*

AIA PUBLISHING

ED LEHNER

Grandpa's Horse and Other Tales
Ed Lehner
Copyright © 2021
Published by AIA Publishing, Australia
ABN: 32736122056
http://www.aiapublishing.com

ISBN: 978-1-922329-27-1

DEDICATION

Thank you to my wife, Julie Ward, for her constant help and encouragement. Thanks to Tahlia Newland at AIA Publishing for agreeing to take on this project. Thanks to Katherine Kirk at Gecko Edit for correcting all my grammatical errors. And thanks to Rose Newland for her awesome cover design and putting up with all my little tweaks.

CONTENTS

GRANDPA'S HORSE

As I remember now, it was the spring of 1946, and I was five years old. The war over, the celebrations done, and folks were back to trying to find some normalcy in their lives after years of fear and sacrifice.

I lived with my mom and dad, my maternal grandfather (fondly called 'Pa' by his family and by some of his closer friends), and our hired man, Tom, who was also my dad's cousin. We lived on a hundred and sixty acres of eastern Iowa farmland. We had sixteen milking cows, a breeding bull, two dozen or so hogs, a chicken house full of chickens and a large family garden. We subsisted on what we raised and grew. Our only income was from selling cream to the local creamery that made butter and cheese. Also, when the hens were laying, upward of thirty-six to forty-eight dozen eggs a week, which were picked up by the creamery truck to be sold in town. It was a lot of hard work. Long twelve-hour days in the hot summer sun. Work and long days didn't let up much, even in the cold Iowa winters.

But then there were the horses which we still used for some of the farm work. We did have a tractor, but my grandfather and a lot of the other farmers still used horses for various farm duties such as pulling hay wagons to the barn and pulling wagons to load shocks of oats for threshing. We had Belgians, a large work horse, but not as big as the Clydesdale we'd see pulling the beer wagon on television.

In late March that year, Pa and my dad went to a Tuesday farm sale. They didn't show up for chores and milking so Tom and I struggled through the feeding, the milking, separating the milk and cream, and cleaning up. We went up to the house for supper.

Pa and Dad were already at the table, slightly inebriated. My dad had a silly grin, Pa was weaving a bit, and Mom was frowning and not speaking.

We sat for supper and Pa announced in his broken English, "Well, by goddammit, we bought new horse today. Truck's bringin' her tomorrow."

Dad just grinned. Mom wasn't speaking.

Cousin Tom said, "On it now, that's a fine thing."

Mom didn't say a word. I was pretty excited. A new horse!

The next day dawned. After chores, at breakfast, Mom still wasn't speaking. The stock truck arrived later that morning. It backed up to the loading chute and out stepped the horse, multicolored brown, black, and white. She was a proud animal, beautiful arch to her strong neck, head held high. Pa led her to her stall in the barn.

The next morning Pa opened the door to the barn and out came a charging large brown, black, and white steed at full gallop. She ran through the barnyard fence, didn't stop until she had taken out two neighbors' fences, and ended up in yet another neighbor's front yard. Pa, Dad, and Tom got in our car, finally tracking her down.

All returned home, two men along with an embarrassed and humble Pa leading the horse from the back window.

Mom definitely wasn't speaking.

Pa put the horse back in the barn, now haltered, salve on her cuts and abrasions, and tied her securely in her stall.

Pa called our neighbors, apologizing as best he could, assuring them that their fences would be repaired. He added, "That goddamned horse will either be taught a goddamned lesson tomorrow morning or it'll break its goddamned neck."

Next morning came, chores were done, breakfast eaten, and Mom still wasn't speaking. It appeared to be time for whatever was about to happen. Pa and

Tom went to the hay mow and carried down about a hundred and fifty feet of one-inch hay rope. Pa proceeded to tie an end between two windows in the eighteen-inch-thick stone barn foundation wall. He carried the other end in through the barn door to the horse stall. He walked back out and into the house.

Word had spread on the party line like a firestorm about Pa's horse, the fences, that something important was about to happen. Neighbors began arriving to watch in anticipation of a possible spectacle that might be unfolding. Bottles were being passed about. Wagers were being made. Children were running about with crazed excitement. The women gossiped together. Tension and anticipation were thick in the air, like a gathering Iowa thunderstorm.

The moment had arrived. Pa walked out of the house, proudly, ramrod straight, into the horse stall. A few minutes later he emerged and held the door open and stood back. A moment later, there emerged a flash of a brown, black, and white locomotive gathering steam with every stride . . . until . . . until the rope ran taut. Everyone gasped, or held their breath.

The two-ton beast, having literally come to the end of its rope, came to an immediate halt, doing a complete ass-over-appetite flip, landing flat on her back. I felt the ground shake when she hit. The onlookers had fallen stone silent. She lay there for a minute, then slowly rolled onto splayed legs, nose on the ground. Finally raising her head and looking around, she turned and walked meekly back into the barn. That horse, eventually named Molly, never did the door rush again.

Suddenly, the crowd came back to life, cheering their approval. Pa closed the barn door and walked over and had pulls from several proffered bottles, shook hands, and exchanged words with a few of the folks, and went into the house for coffee and to read yesterday's newspaper. The crowd slowly broke up and went home.

The event was the topic of stories for years to come with added exaggeration as time went on.

Mom finally started speaking two weeks later.

Seven years later, Dad bought another tractor and the horses were sold. Pa died the year after.

THE LIBRARY OF
THE OCCULT

Emma was walking across the stage for graduation and when she got to the person handing out the degrees, he looked at her and broke into a laugh. Then all the professors and dignitaries on the stage joined in the laughter, pointing at her, and then everyone in the audience joined in and started shouting, "Failure, has-been, loser . . ."

CHAPTER I

She awoke from her recurring dream with a start, her heart pounding. Her doctoral dissertation was in only four months. She still had one more chapter, a vital chapter, to do on her thesis, "Occult Feminine Full Moon Rituals," and desperately needed to research one book to finalize it. But only three copies existed in the whole world that she knew of: two in private collections and the other in the little-known Library of the Occult in London.

Desperate, she hit up her father yet one more time for airfare and lodging for a trip to London. She was now twenty-seven years old and had been working on her higher education for nine years, seven of which were for her PhD at Harvard. His patience and support for her education was growing thin, but still, not without her incessant pleading, he consented. Her flight was now on its final approach to Heathrow.

Early next morning, after a jet-lagged sleep in a less-than-stellar hotel, she found the library after a walk through a once-elegant neighborhood of now old and rundown mansions turned into dingy apartments, with any number of not-yet-opened (due to the early hour) pubs, tattoo parlors, and sad-looking shops lining the way. The library was a small, old, dark, dreary, and tired-looking three-story, probably a onetime manor for some nouveau riche from past times.

She walked up some decaying moss-covered concrete steps to a large wooden front door, then into a musty, dark foyer, hesitating for a moment as her eyes adjusted to the dim light. She approached a desk behind which a woman, neither young nor old, and dressed in a high-collared long-sleeved black dress looking like something from the 1900s, held court. Her gray hair was tied in a bun as severe as the look she gave Emma.

Emma put on a brave smile. "Good morning. I'm wondering if you could help me. I'm looking for the book, *Full Moon Rituals* by Reginald Smythe. I understand you have a copy here?"

The woman looked through an old card file and then disapprovingly back at her. "Yes. We do have a copy, but it is in the restricted area and is available only to a few select patrons and you are not one. Good day."

"But isn't there any possibility of me somehow looking at it? I don't want to remove it from library.

There is one chapter I need for research for my doctoral thesis. Please?" she said, her voice begging.

The woman peered over her glasses and gave her an even colder stare. "What do you not understand? It is not available to you. You are not a select patron. There are only seven patrons allowed access to that room, and I know them all. I am most certain you are not one of them. Now, good day!"

Emma didn't know how to respond to the woman's dismissal. She desperately needed to get a look at that book. She thought of another book, much less rare, and asked if she might be able to look at that one. The woman again looked through the card file, then sharply at Emma. "Yes, you may. It is on the second floor." She huffily gave directions where to find it. "Sign in here."

Emma signed in, needing to give her name, the address where she was staying, home address, and phone number. She then had to show her passport and drivers' license. The woman looked at her proffered documents, wrote down a long list of notes, and then reluctantly allowed her in.

Emma walked to the stairs, feeling the scrutiny of the woman burning like two hot coals into her back. Her heart was racing, but she was in. Now she had to find the restricted area and figure out how to get in.

She walked up the old, once elegant grand

staircase to the second floor and saw dimly lit hallways leading both to her left and right. She went to the left as she was directed. It smelled of dust and old books. She found the door and went into an even mustier room filled with three aisles between bookcases heavy with books. There was no numbering system, but she found the old, mostly leather-bound books were all neatly arranged in alphabetical order. She really had no use whatsoever for that particular one, since she had already read the copy in the Harvard library, but she now had some time to hatch a plan. Around one corner of shelves were two old study desks from a forgotten era. A man was sitting at one. He was old, maybe her grandfather's age, with long white hair that curled over the collar of his white shirt and tweed jacket. He had a well-trimmed white beard and below that she saw a black necktie. He looked up at her over his wire-rimmed glasses with a startled look on his face.

CHAPTER 2

"Oh, I'm so sorry, sir. I didn't mean to scare you," she said, her own eyes wide with surprise. A cold shiver ran down her back.

The old man said in a much younger sounding voice, "You were so quiet. I was so deeply engrossed in this study on herbal tinctures to combat hexes, I didn't hear you. I'm sorry for startling you, young lady. Are you looking for something particular? I am quite familiar with this library and might be able to help."

He had kind eyes and seemed nice, so she explained her dilemma about needing to see a chapter in *Full Moon Rituals*, by Reginald Smythe, for her doctoral thesis and that it was in a restricted room.

"Oh, yes, my dear. I know that book. Miss Pritchard is very protective of her domain here. I may be able to persuade her to let you see it," he said with a warm, paternal smile. "Let me go talk to her."

"I'm so sorry to bother you with this. Really. I'm interrupting your own research."

"It is of no matter. I need to get up and move about for a moment to keep my old body from seizing up completely. I have been sitting here for far too long." He slowly and carefully raised his thin body, using his arms to help him get to his feet. He spent a few moments steadying his balance, rolled his shoulders, and smiled at her. "There, that should do it. I shall return momentarily." And he slowly walked toward the doorway.

She heard him muttering to himself, "I don't know how much longer I can keep going if I don't find that bloody formula."

As she watched him walk away, she wondered how old he really was. Much older than her grandfather, as she had first guessed. She waited at the top of the stairs and heard his raised voice. "I have a perfect right to let her see that book! Please, if your memory might be deserting you—"

The woman replied angrily, "My memory is not deserting me, and please keep your voice down, Mr. Smythe. She may be listening."

Emma's heart began racing and perspiration began to form on her forehead. *Mr. Smythe. No. It can't be him. He's been dead over fifty years. Smythe is a common enough name in England, isn't it? But he said, 'It was mine . . .'* They were now whispering but she knew they were arguing. *This was a bad idea. I should get out of this place. It's starting to creep me out.*

A minute later the whispers ceased, and she heard

the jangle of keys. She saw 'Mr. Smythe' coming slowly up the stairs and she regretted his going down. It looked so difficult for him as he slowly moved up the steps. He finally managed to reach the top, stopping to catch his breath.

"I'm so sorry, sir. The stairs looked very difficult for you. I shouldn't have—"

He raised a hand to quiet her. "It is jolly good. I need some exercise. The truth is, I am not as old as I look. There are circumstances that have gotten out of control, but I shan't trouble you my problems, my dear girl. Pay no heed. Come and follow me."

Her heart was racing from both fear and anticipation. Her instincts were telling her to turn and run down the stairs and get away from this place as fast as she could. This was getting stranger by the minute. She should not have come here. But she had come this far and to see this damn book which now seemed to be within her reach. She followed him down the hallway to the right.

CHAPTER 3

He led her to the last door on the left, took a key ring filled with ancient looking keys, selected one, and unlocked the old oaken door elaborately carved with symbols of the occult. Some she recognized from her research, others she did not. The ones she did know were for protection of the contents within. Mr. Smythe opened the door and ushered her into a room. It reeked of dust and the smell of old books on shelves lining two walls. The room was dimly lit, like everywhere else she had been in this library. He led her to the table and offered her a seat in an old, straight-backed chair, then walked over to a shelf, retrieving a book which he brought back and, with apparent pride, offered to her.

"Here is what you have come so far to see. Take your time. I shall return within the hour and set you free," he said with a reserved chortle. "I must lock the door when I leave. Rules, you know. We wouldn't want to get Miss Pritchard in a huff now, would we?"

"No, no, of course not. Thank you. Please don't forget me." It was more a plea than a request.

"Of course I shan't forget you, my dear girl. As I said, I shall return within the hour." He turned, and went out. She heard the lock click with an ominous sound.

Her heart was racing both with the anxiety of being locked in the room and the fact that what she had traveled a thousand miles to get a look at was lying in front of her. She dove in, found the chapter she was looking for, and began taking copious notes and pictures of some of the more important pages, especially those with old woodcut images. Time flew. She checked her watch. It was now well over an hour since Mr. Smythe had left her. So she continued on researching this book. Time passed. Two hours and nary a sound. She was getting nervous. He's old. Maybe he forgot. But Miss Pritchard knows I'm here.

Her anxiety level continued to rise. She got up and checked the door. Locked. She was a prisoner. She knocked loudly. Nothing. "Anybody out there? I need to leave now." She checked her cell phone. No service. Frantically, she began to pace around the room like a caged animal, looking for what, she hadn't a clue. Maybe a spare key? She checked under the table, under the chairs, everywhere. Nothing. She went to the window. Secured with bars on the outside. Walking back to the table, she mindlessly tapped on the walnut panels on the wall with her knuckles. Tap,

tap, tap. Bonk. Tap, tap, tap. One panel had sounded hollow. She rapped on all the others. Solid. She went back to the hollow-sounding one. *Maybe it's a secret passage. I saw somewhere some of these old houses have secret passages. It might be a way out of here.*

She felt around the trim boards and felt something like a button that clicked when she pushed on it. The panel opened. A cool blast of thick, musty air greeting her surprise. She opened it. Stairs faded into blackness, stairs that led down to where? Freedom? She felt around and found a light switch. A soft yellow glow showed old wooden stairs leading down to a landing. She got her things and carefully started down, hoping against hope she might have found a way out of her prison.

After the landing the stairway turned and led down another flight, now stone steps, to a doorway. She calculated she might now be in the basement. She peeked through the doorway into a stone-walled room about twelve feet square. The one piece of furniture, a table, sat in the center, covered with some old-looking manuscripts. She didn't bother with them, being more interested in a doorway out. She saw a door on one wall but it had been sealed with bricks and mortar. She ran over and pounded and pushed on it but it was solid. She pounded on it, yelling, "Help! Is anyone out there? Please help me!"

Dead silence answered her.

Frustrated, she felt tears start to come. *No! I can't cry. Stay focused.* The manuscripts caught her, lying open on the old wooden table like they had been left in haste. She could tell they were old—very old. She knew she shouldn't touch them but curiosity got the best of her and she pulled a pen from her bag and carefully separated them so she could see them better. They were in Latin, written in an old script including several crude woodblock prints. She had studied both Latin and Greek exactly for this reason, to translate old texts as originally written, not from a translation. The titles roughly translated to something like "Spells for Rapid Aging" and "Reversing Aging."

Distracted momentarily from her dilemma, she pulled out her cell phone and took all the photos she thought she might need to do a thorough translation later, if she ever got out of this prison. Getting the documentation she wanted, but feeling even more defeated, she glumly walked back up the stairs. She had just closed the secret panel when she heard keys jingling outside the door.

"Mr. Smythe? Hey, whoever! I'm locked in here. Please unlock the door. Please!" she called, her request sounding more pathetic than she intended

CHAPTER 4

Akey entered the lock. The door swung open and she saw a man. It wasn't Mr. Smythe. He wore all black, and had a black, pointed beard over a narrow, sallow face with dark, beady eyes that cast a menacing, evil look. "Who are you?" he growled at her, grabbing both her arms.

"I'm a guest of Mr. Smythe. He was supposed to be back to let me out hours ago. I'm doing research for my thesis. Let go of me! Now!" she answered, with rising anger outweighing her fear.

"That bastard Smythe! What are you looking for? How much did he tell you? Did you find it?" he screamed, eyes growing larger as he started to shake her.

"It's none of your damn business if he told me anything." Then in a slow deliberate voice, she said, " Take your goddamn hands off me. Now! I will not ask again."

He just glared at her, tightening his hold, sneering. "I know he's trying to break the spell. Tell me what he said. Did you find it? Tell me!" He continued to shake her.

She stared him in the eyes. "Okay, asshole! I warned you! Enough!"

Emma was not a formidable woman. She looked fairly harmless, with her five-foot-six-inch slight build and unruly shock of curly blond hair. She took three deep breaths, centering her focus, relaxing her body.

Completely relaxed, she said very calmly, "Sorry," and brought all her energy and focus into the upthrust of her arms between his, breaking his grip, simultaneously releasing a quick but deadly centered kick to the man's groin. Her kick was dead-on. Her fists came down solidly on his ears. He looked at her in surprise. His eyes bulged like they might blast out of their sockets. He bent over, blowing out a breath. His hands moved to his groin area. Emma then took a step back and executed a snap kick to his nose, hearing bone crack, seeing blood immediately spurting out. Not finished, she spun on her right foot, left leg cocked to release another devastating kick to the side of his head, sending him to the floor in a crumpled heap, retching and gasping for air. Then he went limp and his breathing slowly quieted. Good. Guess I didn't kill the asshole. I warned him.

She struggled and dragged his limp body all the way into the room, calmly gathered her things, and closed and locked the door behind her. There was no one behind the reception desk. Wondering what had happened to Miss Pritchard, but not really caring, she left the building, found the right key and locked the front door, dropped the keys through the mail slot, and walked back to her hotel, wondering what had just happened.

Remembering Miss Pritchard had her lodging information, she checked out of her hotel, fearful that that guy might know more wackos and send them looking for her. She walked three London blocks and found another hotel. While more upscale and expensive than she wanted, she didn't care. She knew she'd be safer there.

CHAPTER 5

Securely in her room, she ran a tub of water with some bubble bath from the array of soaps and lotions provided by the hotel. She got two of the small bottles of chardonnay from the minibar and settled in to soak away this strange day.

Her brain finally settling down, she thought back to growing up in Salem, Massachusetts, and her early childhood obsession with the Salem witch trails that took place there in the late 1600s. From her early years, she had read any book on the subject she could find. She had studied history in college, with the sole purpose of going on to earn a PhD in history with a focus on witchcraft, so that she might dispel the myths surrounding it, especially with the myths surrounding so-called witches.

Two bottles finished, she showered off, dressed, and went out to a nearby pub for some dinner. Famished, she downed a huge order of fish and chips and two pints. Satiated and slightly tipsy, she went to her room, stripped, and fell into bed, soon enjoying a dreamless sleep.

In the morning she felt like a new person. She wondered how to kill time until her early evening flight home the next day. After a continental breakfast and two cups of rich coffee at the hotel, the day before came tumbling back to her and she began to worry about that man. Deep down, she felt a little sorry that she might have done more injury to him than just breaking his nose. She got out her cell and called the library.

The familiar voice of Miss Pritchard answered. "Library of the Occult. How may I help you?"

"Hi, Miss Pritchard. This is Emma Morgan from yesterday. Remember me?"

"Of course, of course. Oh, my dear girl, I must apologize for leaving you locked in that room," she said with a hasty and much friendlier tone than the day before. "Mr. Smythe took ill and we had to rush him to the hospital. I wanted to return to release you, but Mr. Smythe has no one else, so I felt I should be with him until he was settled. Then when I returned and scurried up to open the door for you, I found that dreadful Sylvester Arnon on the floor lying in his blood and vomit. He was moaning something about a she-devil from hell. I again called for an ambulance that would hopefully take him to another hospital than where Mr. Smythe was residing. Such a disturbing day, oh my. They are arch enemies, you know."

"No, I had no idea," Emma was able to interject.

"No. Of course, my dear. How could you? Did Mr. Arnon release you?"

"Yes, he did. The poor man. What happened to him?" she asked, over-feigning her innocence.

"We have no idea. I thought you might know something," Miss Pritchard said, her voice dripping with innocence, and rising into a question like she already knew the answer, like Emma's mother did when Emma was being naughty. "Whatever did happen to him, he would have most certainly deserved it. He is a truly wretched man. He is beyond arrogant, thinking he is so much superior to any other mortal, claiming he is a warlock of highest order. It is rumored he practices the 'dark arts.' Are you sure you know nothing, maybe about some she-devil?"

"No. Oh no. He opened the door and I left," Emma answered, again overdoing her feigned innocence.

"I'm sure you don't," Miss Pritchard said with a slight chuckle. "Thank you, my dear girl. I'm not sure how you did what you did, but my lips shan't ever utter another word of this event."

Emma could almost see her doing the zipper thing across her lips.

"Miss Morgan, would you please call Mr. Smythe?

He was quite worried about you, leaving you like he did. It would make him feel much better if he heard from you."

"I'd be happy to. Can I contact him at the hospital?"

"Most certainly." She gave Emma a number to call and the location.

They said their goodbyes and Emma called the hospital and was quickly connected to his room. He picked up.

"Hello, Mr. Smythe. This is Emma Morgan. We met yesterday at the library and you let me into that restricted room to research a book for my dissertation."

"Of course I remember you, my dear girl. I apologize for taking ill and leaving you locked in there. I do hope Miss Pritchard found you well."

I am really tired of being called 'dear girl.' "Well, it's a long story, sir."

"I have nothing but time, being stuck in this infernal hospital. Doctors say I must stay for observation. However, I must say, no one seems to be doing much observing. So please, continue your story."

She told him the saga of her day, leaving out any mention of Sylvester Arnon, not disputing his idea that Miss Pritchard had been the one to let her out of the room. On a roll, she told him about the secret panel and subsequently discovering the manuscripts. When she mentioned the titles, she heard him suck in a deep breath.

"Oh, dear Miss Morgan, could you please bring those over to me? It would be such a favor. Truly it would."

"I left them undisturbed. They were very old, fragile parchment. But I took photos of them, thinking I might translate them someday."

"You could translate them? Could you do it straight away?"

"It might take a while, and my flight out is tomorrow. I don't think I have the time. Maybe after I get back home and finish my thesis."

"If you would do so now, I would compensate you handsomely for your services. I shall also pay all expenses you incur from your stay. Knowing the contents of these is extremely important to me. Extremely important! I beg of you, my dear Miss Morgan, to indulge me. My life depends on it. I promise I shall make it well worth your while."

She heard the panic in his voice. "I'll have to think about it. I'll take a look and see what would be involved. Some of these old manuscripts are easier than others to translate. Can I call you back?"

"Of course, of course," he replied breathlessly. "Please consider my offer. It is of the utmost importance to me. I will be waiting to hear from you. Thank you. You have no idea how important these manuscripts are to me."

CHAPTER 6

She said goodbye and clicked off, still hanging on to her cell, considering his offer. She had all she needed for her missing chapter to her thesis, mainly due to the kindness of this man. *He said his life depended on these translations.* Surely she could stay a little longer, since he had promised to pay for her whole time here. He seemed sincere and, hopefully, honest. She would have plenty of time to finish her thesis now, since she had what she needed for her final chapter. She wanted to check out the extent of what would be needed for the translations, so she emailed the photos from her phone to herself so they would be on her laptop and easier to work with. She skimmed them and decided two, maybe three days, tops. *He said he'd pay me. Handsomely? Sure. Why not?*

She called him back. "Sorry to bother you again, Mr. Smythe, but you said you'd pay my expenses plus pay me handsomely. Exactly how handsomely are you thinking?"

He laughed. "I appreciate your candor, Miss Morgan. The translations and manuscripts would be worth . . . Would fifty thousand US dollars be adequate compensation for your troubles?"

She gasped. "Oh no, no! That is far too much."

"My dear Miss Morgan, what this would mean to me is priceless. Covering your expenses plus fifty thousand dollars is the least I can do. It shall give you some spending money to tide you over. I can certainly afford it for this service you are performing for me. You have no idea. I will make a bank transfer or write a check, as you prefer. I shall do it straight away. Do you have your bank's routing number and your account number? There are pen and paper right here on my side table."

She was speechless. He was serious. That was more money than she'd ever had in her life. She swallowed, dug in her bag for her checkbook and gave him the information he would need for the transfer. He could drain her account with this information, but there was no money in it anyway. Her voice was trembling. "This should do it for the bank transfer, if you are truly serious."

"I am deadly serious. I shall make the transfer immediately. Check your account in about an hour. Please keep track of all of your expenses, including your airfare, and I shall compensate you when you give me that amount. Thank you again. I must go now. I am supposed to be resting now." He chuckled and clicked off.

Emma called the airline and was able to change her flight for three days from now, to be safe.

She got out her laptop, pencil, and notepad and went to work. She was able to isolate the block prints and printed them in the hotel business suite.

An hour later, curious, she checked her bank account and it showed a deposit of fifty thousand dollars. *My god, he trusts me to do this for him and not just disappear. Who is this man?*

She worked into the night, ordering in food. After a restless sleep, she had a continental breakfast from the hotel and several cups of coffee. By six that night she had finished translations of what she considered to be something that made absolutely no sense to her whatsoever, but she was sure of her work. With a sigh of accomplishment, she called Mr. Smythe to tell him the news and that she'd drop the translations off at the hospital in the morning. He was elated, but he was presently being released from his confinement, as he called it.

He asked, "Where are you staying? I shall send a car for you at ten tomorrow morning."

"Might I ask where I'll be taken?"

"Of course, of course." He gave her the address of his home.

She gave him the address of the hotel and they

disconnected, she with a sigh of relief, but not without a knot of anxiety in her gut. She looked up his address and it was an estate on the edge of London. What was she dealing with here? There was this Mr. Smythe, then that crazy man, secret passages, manuscripts of spells. She went to the minibar and got three more little bottles of wine and ran a hot tub to soak in and gather her thoughts. After another dinner of fish and chips and two more pints, she fell into a restless sleep.

CHAPTER 7

At ten o'clock the next morning, she was nervously waiting in front of the hotel when an older Rolls-Royce pulled up. A uniformed chauffeur got out. "Would you be Miss Morgan?"

"Yes. That's me."

"My name is Jeffers. Mr. Smythe sends his apologies for not meeting you in person, but he has been strictly ordered to rest. You appear to be prepared to go, then."

Jeffers took her bags. She took a breath and got into the luxurious car.

"Please help yourself to the tea and pastries." They were spread before her. "I shall get you champagne, if you so wish."

"No champagne, thank you. Tea will be fine."

"As you wish, miss."

She tried to relax into the plush seat, but was so filled with apprehension she couldn't touch the pastries or tea.

After a forty-five-minute drive under ominous, cloudy skies that threatened rain, Jeffers turned into a driveway, stopped in front of a large iron gate, and punched in a code. The gates swung open slowly to reveal a treelined drive to a magnificent house, somewhere between a medieval castle and a small hotel.

Jeffers stopped the car at the front entrance and opened her door, escorting her to a formidable front door, quickly opened by a middle-aged no-nonsense-looking woman in a maid's uniform. She took Emma's bag from Jeffers and said, "Miss Morgan, I am Miss Grant. I shall take you to the study. Please follow me."

Emma followed two paces behind down a parquet-floored hallway. She was awed by the luxurious magnificence of the house. Paintings, sculptures, and the requisite suits of old armor lined the hall. She was directed into a dark-paneled room with a large, orderly desk, plush leather chairs, a thick carpet, and copious bookshelves filled with leather-bound volumes. Where there weren't bookshelves, there was expensive looking artwork. Tall windows flooded the room with the pending storm. A bolt of lightning flashed, followed by a roll of thunder. Two bouquets of flowers brightened the room, giving the room a sweet fragrance and some reassurance to Emma. Miss Grant showed her to a seat with a side table set with more tea and small sandwiches. She was too nervous now to even consider eating anything.

A moment later, Mr. Smythe slowly entered the room from another door. She rose to greet him but he motioned her to stay seated. He looked more pale and wan than when they had first met only a few days ago.

"Miss Morgan, I am so happy you came. Thank you. I owe you a deep gratitude." He sat slowly and carefully in a chair opposite her.

His fragile presence quickly dissipated her fears. "I'm happy to be of service, Mr. Smythe. And please, call me Emma."

"Ah yes, formalities. Please call me Alexander, or Alex will do just fine. You said you made the translations?" he asked eagerly.

"Yes, yes. I printed copies for you of both the original Latin and the translations, along with enlarged images of the block prints. It should all be there," she said as she handed him a sheaf of paper.

"Splendid, splendid." He quickly went through the papers. When he was finished, she noticed his lips quivering, tears forming in his eyes. He quickly looked away, shaking his head as though trying to shake away his emotions. Regaining his composure, he turned back to her and said with a shaky voice, his eyes shining with moisture, "This is it. This is what I have been searching for. Perfect. Thank you, Miss—I mean, Emma. I cannot express my gratitude for what you have done for me."

"I'm happy this is what you wanted. And thank you for your generosity. This was all quite an adventure, quite an adventure."

"Yes, quite an adventure, indeed. Now, Emma, do you have your receipts so I may cover them as I promised?"

"I forgot to bring them, but may I email them to you?"

"Of course. Here is my card with my contact information. And please do, at your earliest convenience. Now, I would love to stay and chat, but I think my doctor was quite serious about me needing rest. I must lie down and read this treasure you have found. If this works as it should, you have truly saved this old man. Miss Grant will be showing you out. Jeffers will return you to your hotel. If you will please excuse me, now."

Slowly and with unsteady legs, he rose from the chair. She leaped up to help, but he waved her off. "I am fine." He stood before her, looking deeply into her eyes. She looked back and, for a moment, got a glimpse of the handsome man he must have been in his youth.

"Oh, one more thing, Emma. I talked to Miss Pritchard today and she said that Mr. Arnon had been hospitalized after an incident at the library. Would you happen to know anything about that? Something about a she-devil from hell," he said with a smirk.

"Me? No. Of course not. Why would you think that?" she answered, all too hastily.

Now his smirk had turned into a broad grin. "Just asking. Thank you again, Emma." His look was with a tenderness that made her melt a bit inside and she thought about hugging him but quickly dismissed the idea. They shook hands. He turned and went back through the door he had entered from. Miss Grant magically appeared to escort her out to the front door where Jeffers awaited.

CHAPTER 8

Six months later Emma walked proudly across the stage to receive her PhD in Historical Studies from Harvard University. Her dissertation had received high praise from her graduate committee. Her major professor was urging her to expand it into a book. Her family was in the audience and after the ceremony they all hovered around in the lobby of the auditorium, congratulating her and chatting.

She noticed a well-dressed and handsome young man standing outside the circle of her well-wishers, trying to catch her eye. After things were quieting down with her family, he again caught her eye. He looked strangely familiar, but she couldn't place him. She excused herself and went to where he was standing.

"Do I know you?" she asked.

"I am so sorry to intrude," he said with a formal British accent, and a voice she vaguely recognized from her trip six months ago.

He continued, "I was impelled to come to your ceremony and congratulate you on your great success.

I am truly honored to be here, albeit a gate-crasher."

"You did not answer my question," she said with an edge to her voice.

"Ah, yes. Where are my manners? But I am reluctant to tell you. You may not readily accept what I have to tell you. But please, my name is Smythe. Alexander Smythe. But please, Alex will do just fine."

She sucked in a breath. "So you're Mr. Smythe's son?"

"No, I am the son of Ronald Smythe."

Her eyes popped wide open and she brought a hand to her mouth as she exclaimed more loudly than she'd intended, "No! You're not! No! Surely you're not! You're not the gentleman I met six months ago, not the Alexander Smythe? Surely you . . . No! No, it's not possible!"

Her thoughts flew back to the library and manuscripts about aging spells and Sylvester Arnon. It all came together. She felt unsteady and put her other hand against the wall for support. He quickly grabbed her and helped her to steady herself.

"I'm so sorry to spring this on you like this."

She took two deep breaths. "It's okay. This can't be true. I'm okay now. This isn't true." She slowly regained her equilibrium. "I'm okay now, I think. You can let go." He released his hold and stood back.

"Ah, I am sorry, but yes, it most certainly is very

true. Those documents you gave me on the aging spells, they were thankfully what I needed. I, with the help of some of my comrades, of course, managed to reverse the spell. The Mr. Arnon you met at the library was responsible for casting that spell upon me, causing me to age almost overnight into an eighty-five-year-old man."

He continued by saying that Arnon had been disgraced, summarily banned from the library, and shunned by anyone who knew him. He had disappeared and he was rumored to be in India, where he had entered a Buddhist monastery.

Continuing, he said, "Six weeks ago several others of the select library members and myself found the secret passageway you told me about. With further investigation, we discovered yet another hidden chamber you missed, containing many other such ancient parchments with similar spells and alchemy. Arnon must have discovered it, never telling anyone. All those documents have now been sealed away in a completely secure vault while they are being studied by some occult scholars. They shall never see the light of day and will be never again used for such treachery."

She sank back onto a bench, taking some deep breaths and several moments to process all she had just heard. He saw her dismay and said, "My sincere apologies. I do hope I am not causing you any unwarranted distress on this illustrious day. I wanted to come to congratulate you on your success and give you a gift. I am happy I was of service in your accomplishment."

"No. No, it's okay. It's just that, I don't know. My studies of the occult have always been with the idea that this stuff was no more than wishful thinking and mythology."

"Ah, far from mythology, my dear Emma. It is all quite real. I again apologize for taking you from your family and friends. I should leave now."

She was confused and she wanted to talk more with this man. "No. Please. Come and join us. We are going for a celebration dinner and party. Please come. I want to talk more with you about, well, everything. It's a lot for me to process. It was good of you to come today. How did you know? Get in?"

"Let's just say, I know people who know people. Oh, I almost forgot. Here is a present for you. Please wait until later to open it," he said as he handed her a tightly sealed envelope. "Are you sure I won't be an inconvenience?"

"Not at all. You will be very welcome." She took him back to her group and introduced him only as the man who was instrumental to her finalizing her thesis.

Later that night, alone in her apartment, she opened his envelope. Along with a thank you/ congratulation note, she saw a cash transfer into her bank account of one million dollars. She again sat in stunned disbelief, dropping the envelope and note, immobile for several minutes. Shaky, she managed to get to her computer and checked her bank balance. $1,027,767.39. It took a long time for her heart to quit pounding. Sometime later she was calm enough to fall into a deep sleep, waking in the morning still in disbelief.

CHAPTER 9

Emma had invited Alex to meet the next morning for breakfast at a small café close to her apartment by the Harvard campus. Instead of his formal tailored suit, he was in sneakers, jeans, and a light V-necked sweater, his once feeble body looking strong and fit. *He really is handsome, she thought, giving him a once-over.*

Once seated and their order taken, Emma first thanked him for his present and then adamantly refused his gift.

Alex would not hear of it. "You were paramount in giving me my life back, for actually saving my life, restoring me to my youth. That is a small token of my appreciation. My gratefulness is beyond anything I could ever offer you."

She considered this and nodded her head in defeat. Then she had nothing but questions which rolled out nonstop.

"Whoa," he said, "one at a time. I shall start at the beginning." He went on to tell how his and Arnon's great-grandfathers were best of friends growing up. The magical and alchemical arts had been practiced by both families for many generations. Alex's family had accumulated great wealth over the years from worldwide business interests to which he was now the only remaining heir and solely in charge of managing. The families had remained close until Alex's great-grandfather, Reginald, wrote his book, *Full Moon Rituals*. Sylvester Arnon's great-grandfather then claimed, without any merit, that it was his research on this very topic and Reginald had stolen all his work for his own purpose and had the book published. That incident caused a fracture in the relationship between the families and they became enemies, the feud carrying through until present day.

Sylvester Arnon had taken it upon himself to settle the score once and for all when he discovered the manuscripts containing the 'aging spells.' He successfully performed the spell, sending Alex into rapid aging from a vital twenty-eight-year-old to someone well into his eighties or beyond. Thankfully, the spell slowed incrementally as the aging process increased, or he would have been dead some time ago. Emma, of course, had found the manuscripts, and Alex and his friends were able to reverse the process. The whole ordeal had taken a toll on him from which he was now almost fully recovered.

Their food had arrived. "That is it, all in a nutshell. What you consider to be myth is something that is quite real and not to be taken lightly. Now, let us enjoy our food."

"Of course."

As they quietly ate for a few minutes, she noticed him stealing glances at her, making her smile inside.

She interrupted between bites. "I should tell you, I'll be heading back to England next month for a more extended stay. I've been granted a postdoctoral position at Cambridge for at least a year. So we'll sort of be neighbors."

"How perfectly wonderful, Emma! Congratulations. May I call upon you for dinner sometime? We must exchange our contact information."

Her heart skipped a beat. "Of course. I would like that."

"Meanwhile, I will be spending at a week here in your lovely city, and I would be so happy if you would be my tour guide, but only if you are free to do so," he said, taking a bite of sausage and egg.

"Of course I would. I'd be honored, but only a week? There's a lot to see and enjoy here," she said.

"Of course. I could certainly extend my visit, to see everything you might want to show me, if you so wish," his smile brightening with anticipation.

"I look forward to it," she said with an even bigger smile.

A Man Called
Thomas

Sara awoke with a start. She began shaking her husband. "Wake up Andy. Something's not right."

"What? What're you talking about?" he replied, groggy and irritated. "What do you mean, something's wrong? What time is it? The sun's not even up yet."

Sara responded, "It's five and something's not right. I can feel it. Would you go out and check to make sure things are okay?"

Andy grumbled something about it being too early to get up and his needing coffee. He dressed and went outside, returning fifteen minutes later, now sounding more irritated. "Everything's fine. I looked all around. The garden is good. Chickens are fine."

"I'm still uneasy, Andy. Something's not right."

"You'll feel better after some coffee. Since I'm up so early, I'm going to run to town after I eat something. I need to get some fuel for the tractor. I'm hoping we get delivery on that electric tractor soon. It's taking forever. Anything you need?"

"Stop by Natural Foods and get some ghee and yogurt. And see if there's any news on the fires. I notice less smoke today. Last I heard, they had around seventy percent contained. I'm hoping for rain and an end to this drought."

After he had breakfast and with his second cup of coffee now in his travel mug, Andy jumped into their electric pickup and headed to town.

***

Two hours later Andy rushed into the house, out of breath, and shouted, "Sara! The town's completely deserted! Nobody's there! Nobody!"

"What're you talking about?" responded Sara. "Deserted? That's absurd. Did you go to the grocery store?"

"I did. But nobody was there. Shelves were stocked, meat counter full, veggies seemed fresh. I called out, but it was . . . well, it was completely deserted. I went in the back. No one there. I got what we needed and left a note by the cash register for what I got. It was the same at the gas station. The pumps worked, but no one was there. Then I checked around town. Cars were in driveways or on the street, but no people. Nothing. What the hell's going on? It's like twelve hundred people all just . . . I don't know . . . just disappeared."

Sara responded, "Did you eat some of those mushrooms again? Hallucinating like you always do when you do that? You know it pisses me off when you get this way. Especially driving."

"I did not do any mushrooms!" he said defensively. "I swore off them after the last incident. Come on, let's go in. You'll see."

She glared at him. "You're acting nuts, Andy. I'm not going to town. What the hell's wrong with you?"

Exasperated, he replied, "Please. Just come with me. I'll show you I'm not crazy."

***

Andy had been a hedge fund manager on Wall Street until three years ago, when he and his wife, Sara, a junior attorney on her way to partner at a large corporate law firm, took a summer vacation in Colorado. Both fell in love with the mountains and the peace there.

After returning to their hectic life in New York, they started to find it had become less rewarding, and they both were feeling confined after their visit to the open spaces of the West. On his way to work one morning, Andy bought a Mother Earth News magazine at the newsstand where he bought his usual morning paper. Looking through it reminded him of growing up on the farm in upstate New York.

Sara, from a small town in Ohio, was beginning to realize how much she missed the quieter lifestyle of her youth. After careful and thoughtful consideration, they decided they needed change and elected to shed their careers and big city life and move to Colorado. There, they would try to find some land and start a small farm, raising vegetables and such for farmers' markets and whatever other venues they might find for selling what they hoped to grow.

After telling their parents, all their friends, and their coworkers about their plans, and with everyone thinking they had completely lost their minds, they sold almost everything they owned and headed off to a new life.

Three months later they found the ideal land: fifteen irrigated acres in the southwestern corner of the state. The area had not been on their radar. They were hoping to be closer to metropolitan Denver. But the scarcity of land and high prices sent them farther and farther away, to this location. Their land was five miles outside of the small town of Johnston, an eight hour trip from Denver.

Both had made good salaries in their work and had a goodly sum in a savings account, along with stocks and bonds, and they were able to buy and make the necessary upgrades to the property while remaining free and clear of debt. There was a vintage but well-built and sturdy ranch house, along with several outbuildings, all needing repair, and a broken-down corral. It was the onetime family homestead of a now defunct ranch, most of it sold off over the years in small parcels for homes or small horse properties. No one had lived there in over ten years.

The first few months were spent cleaning up and repairing the buildings and upgrading the house, especially the kitchen and the one bathroom. Solar panels now lined the south-facing ranch house and with the batteries, they could effectively be off the grid. Tall fences were erected to keep out hungry deer and other critters. They purchased a small Kubota tractor, outfitted with a tiller, and a blade for snow removal.

They found the independent-minded people in the surrounding area warm, welcoming, and helpful. There were a number of independent organic farmers in and around the area. There were several larger communities within an hour's drive, with local food co-ops and farmers' markets. The area was teeming with good, healthy food sources and they were assured, if they wanted, there was a good market for more.

After the first year of learning the ropes about climate, growing season, and water management—far different from what they knew from their experience growing up in the East—they managed to have their first productive garden. It was small, for sure, but productive enough to be able to have a booth at one of the farmers' markets with enough salable fare. They were proud of their accomplishments from their hard work.

***

"What the hell? You're right. Where is everybody? Stop! There's Jason's dog."

She rolled down the window and called out, "Buster. Hey, Buster. Come here, boy."

The beagle, recognizing her voice from all the times they visited their friends, Jason and Mary Larson, bounded over to the truck, acting happy to see someone. Sara opened the door and Buster jumped in.

"Let's go by the Larsons' and drop Buster off. They should be home."

They drove a few blocks to the Larsons'. Sara took Buster to the door and knocked. No answer. She opened the unlocked door and called out, to dead silence. She went in and looked around. Everything looked normal, but the house was completely deserted.

She walked back to the truck, now trying to keep herself from total panic. Buster happily jumped in with them again, and they drove around town, stopping by several houses of people they knew. No one was there. No one was anywhere.

Sara got out her cell phone. She had service and called a friend, another farmer about five miles from their place.

Sue answered after a few rings. "Hi Sara, I was just thinking of you."

"Hey Sue, are you folks okay?" Sara asked quickly.

"Yeah," she answered sounding puzzled by the question and the urgency in Sara's voice. "Why?"

"Andy and I are in town and it's completely deserted. I mean, there are no people. Truly, nobody . . . anywhere. I found our friends' dog roaming around loose but there's no one home."

"What're you talking about? No one? Why would that be? A whole town can't just disappear. I don't understand."

"Seriously, we checked everywhere. We checked several of our friends' places and there's nobody there. Everybody's gone."

"Are you home?" Sue asked.

"We're heading there now, after getting some dog food."

Sue said, "We'll head your way. We need to talk."

Sara called her parents in Ohio. There was no answer, and she left a message to call as soon as they could. She called Andy's parents. Again, no answer. Now she was getting really frightened. She called her old law office. It was as if no one had gone to work that day.

Twenty minutes later, Sue and her wife, Ella, came in with a cloud of dust. Sara saw them coming and ran out to meet them.

Ella jumped out. "We drove through town. You're right. It's deserted. Where'd everyone go?"

Sara, now almost hysterical, replied, "I just called everyone I know from out East and no one answered."

Andy came running out. "I just checked online news and there's no updates for today. I checked on my cell and there's only yesterday's news. What the hell's going on?"

They went in the house and sat looking at each other with blank, frightened stares. There was a knock at the door. Andy went to open it, finding a man dressed in a dark suit and tie who had somehow appeared. There was a strange, ethereal glow about him.

"May I come in?" he asked in a deep, resonant

voice, appearing to choose these words of a simple question carefully.

Wondering what anyone was doing out here dressed like this, and how he had gotten there, Andy reluctantly invited him in.

"Greetings, everyone," the man said slowly and shyly, like he was practicing new words he had just learned. "I apologize for intruding. I must explain some things you may be finding . . . strange?

"You may call me Thomas. I am not from here. I am from far away. There is no reason to . . . to be . . . to be frightened. I think that is correct?"

Andy was still standing. The others sat staring at this well-dressed stranger who had this aura about him.

"Where are you from, then," asked Sue. "Why are you glowing?"

Thomas smiled faintly at that. "When I say I am not from here, I mean I am not of this planet, or even this galaxy you call the Milky Way. Is that right? The Milky Way?"

They all nodded with their eyes getting bigger at the story they were hearing.

"This is not my normal form. My normal form, you would not understand. I assumed this human form only two days ago and am still getting used it. Please excuse my clumsiness." He smiled. It appeared to require some work on his part. And then he continued, "I and many others have come here to save this planet. All but a few residents have been removed. We left select ones like you, who truly care for this planet. This planet you call Earth is a very important part of the universe, and it is dying due to the greed, selfishness, and apathy of so many. The unaware and uncaring are the ones who have been removed. They have not been harmed but have been relocated to various other worlds for retraining."

He continued, sounding now like this was well rehearsed. "Earth, as you call it, was to be a planet of choice, where residents were to have the freedom to determine who they would partner with, how they would earn livings, how they might grow in spirit, and how to live gently on this planet that offered so much. Regretfully, we did not realize so many would fall into a pattern of greed, selfishness, fear, and false judgment, killing, war, and religious ideology. It was a great mistake on our part. We have tried to change things, working in the background to help inhabitants change. This did not work. We could wait no longer, as too many people were rapidly killing this once beautiful and bountiful place.

"Thank you for listening so well. I only learned your language two of your Earth days ago. It is getting better, do you agree?" he said with an easier, wider smile.

All were sitting in rapt attention. They nodded vigorously with their eyes wide with fear and wonder.

The man called Thomas continued, "I am here to help in any manner you wish. There are several other families in this valley pod. Be assured, you are not alone. There are many others who were chosen to remain, but only those who care for this planet. Our task is to help you all nurture and restore it. Are you up for this task?"

Again, all nodded vigorously. Sara then asked, "But our parents, families, and friends. What will happen to them? Is this like the end of the world or something?"

"No, it is not the end, but a new beginning. Some, like your parents, will be returned in due course. But many will never be allowed to return so the planet may recover and purify itself, which we shall help it to do. There were too many people, too many who had no regard for the earth and continued to overpopulate, pollute, and abuse the planet. Much will depend on their retraining and willingness to change their lives. No one will suffer harm or injury, and they will reside for retraining somewhere in the many places in the many universes where humans can live."

"Many universes?" asked Sue. "Many? How many are there?"

"There are an infinite amount of what you call universes. There is no end. Some are old, some new, constantly dying and regenerating, like all life. It is much to grasp. But I must go now. I must talk with others."

"Will we see you again? What should we do?" asked a frightened Ella.

The man called Thomas answered, "I shall return soon, and often, to help guide you. You should go on as normal. Grow food. Tend to your lives. You are safe from any harm. We have left many new thinkers to help with new technologies that, along with our guidance, will be free of the vested interests of the past so you may soon thrive without the pollution of old technologies. We will maintain your infrastructure, as we can, but you will most likely not need much of it very soon. It will be quickly made obsolete. I will be back often and will work with you to create a new paradigm. Do not worry. I shall return soon, after I visit some others."

With that, the man called Thomas walked out the door. Andy followed and watched him disappear into a bright flash of light. "He's gone. Just like that. Poof," he said slowly.

Ella was softly crying in Sue's arms.

Sara said flatly, "So this is it, the way the world ends. With a new beginning. It all ends with a new beginning . . . a new . . . beginning."

THE TEST

Willow's heart was racing. *What have I done? God, Willow, you are so stupid. Why did you agree to that? Just because he's a tall, good-looking, star point guard for the basketball team. How dumb can you be? He doesn't care a hoot about me, but I agreed. Shit! Shit! Shit!*

She walked out of the empty classroom after her ALP college-level calculus class. Alex had pulled her aside and asked if she would take the midterm senior calculus test for him. The test was still experimental. It would be done on their computers with assigned codes and passwords for each student. The test could be completed anytime in a two-day period. He seemed to have it all worked out. She would use his computer and he would be there with her, just in case.

"I really need this grade for my scholarship," he had said. "I want to get into med school," he had said. And she got all gaga.

"Yes," she had said. He thanked her, turned, and

walked away to join his friends. It was cheating, pure, plain, and simple. Cheating.

Whereas Alex was super popular, Willow was the opposite. She had one friend, Mary, who was equally unpopular. Willow considered herself neither beautiful nor ugly, but simply considered herself as being plain, with a wild shock of unruly auburn hair and green eyes with flecks of brown. On the other hand, she was smart—very smart. And so was Mary, neither beautiful nor ugly, but smart. Both girls had managed to ride below the radar of their peers, staying away from social media and all the high school drama. Willow was tall, which didn't help, but she mantained a low profile and nobody really knew who she was. She was especially good at math sciences and was planning on studying physics at Stanford, where she had earned an academic scholarship . . . Three months until graduation.

***

Her stomach was in turmoil and she could barely eat her dinner that night.

"Are you okay, honey?" her mother asked. "You've hardly touched your food."

"I'm sorry, Mom. I'm just not that hungry."

Her father chimed in. "Something must

be bothering you. You always have an appetite for meatloaf."

"Just not tonight, Dad. I'm sorry, but can I be excused, please?"

Her two little brothers chimed in, of course, with taunts, until their mother gave them a look, which was enough for them to shut up.

Her parents' concern went on for a few more minutes and she was finally able to escape to her room, citing a load of homework. She flopped onto her bed and hugged her old teddy bear from her childhood. She still always found comfort in that silly old threadworn bear. She didn't sleep well that night, and by morning, she thought she might have a solution.

She and Alex were in the same classic literature class during last period that morning. She caught up with him when he was leaving and pulled him aside.

"I need to talk to you," she said.

He gave her a questioning scowl. "You're not going to back out of our deal, are you?"

She mustered up all the courage she could and said, "Yes and no. I can't cheat for you, but I'll be happy to tutor you. You're smart. I know you are. You're in several ALP science classes, so I know you are. You can master this calculus. I know you can. You know it, you just don't realize you know it. I'll help. Please let me. I can't cheat. If we're caught, our scholarships will be history. And they spot monitor the test with facetime so I can't do this. We'll get into serious trouble. Please?"

He looked at her, thinking this through. "You're right. It was stupid of me to ask you to do that for me. I'm sorry. But, seriously? You'd help me? Why, after I asked you to cheat for me? Why'd you ever agree to do that in the first place?"

"I was taken off guard. I'm not the most popular girl, as you know, and, well, I was thrilled that you even noticed me, and, I don't know, I said yes before I thought of all the ramifications. If you do the work, you can do this. I'm making it my mission for you to ace that test. Okay?"

He hesitated and said, "Okay then, when do we start? And where?"

"This afternoon, after your basketball practice. The local library has study rooms. I go there a lot. It's a good place away from distractions like my mom and little brothers. What time can you make it?"

"If I get showered and don't mess around, I could be there by four."

"See ya then."

***

Alex showed up at four sharp, his black hair still wet from his shower.

"Good practice?" Willow asked.

"Usual. Yeah, it was good, I guess. Game Friday night. You coming?"

"Ah, I hadn't planned on it. Did you bring your notebook and computer?" she said, to change the subject.

"Well, yeah . . . Of course I did." He gave her a look of disbelief at her question.

"Sorry. Stupid question. Let's get started. Where do think you need the most help?"

He went through what he felt he understood and then what he didn't have a clue about, which was a lot.

"So it looks like we have some work to do, then," she said. "So let's get going."

They both realized at the same time that it was 5:30, all of a sudden. Time had flown.

"Oh my god! I have to get going or I'll be late for dinner," she blurted out.

"Oh crap. Me too. Hey, thanks a lot. In just this time, I think some of this is beginning to make sense. Same time tomorrow, then?"

"Yep. See ya then."

Willow had a bigger appetite and slept very well that night.

***

They met after school every afternoon that first week. At school it was still the same. He ignored her and she him, but when they were working together at the library, it was different. He was a really nice guy. And funny. Willow had never dated, but as the days went on, she increasingly looked forward to seeing him.

"So, Willow? That's an interesting name," he said one afternoon.

"Yeah. It's weird, but so are my parents. They are the progeny of some hippies from up north. I guess weird names run in the family. Mom's name is Autumn Dawn and Dad's is Indigo Peace. 'Autumn' and 'Indy' for short, just like Indiana Jones. Go figure. But they seem pretty normal. Dad's a professor in math science over at the university. I guess that's where I get my math brains. And Mom's a psychologist and a counselor at the women's center."

He gave her a warm smile. His dark eyes were sparkling. "Your parents sound interesting. I'd like to meet them sometime. Tell me, Willow, I hardly ever see you around, like you're hiding? You're really pretty cool."

She about fell out of her chair and knew she was blushing from the tips of her toes to the ends of her auburn hair. She swallowed. "I'm painfully shy, Alex.

I am afraid of being around more that one or two people at a time. I'm not very secure with myself." *Why am I telling him this? He'll really think I'm a loser.*

"Yeah, I can understand that. I'm not too happy around crowds either. I feel most at home on the basketball court. But I manage somehow."

"God, Alex! You date Mandy Johnson, the most popular girl in school. And you have friends coming out your ears."

"Yeah, I know. But you want to know something? I'm happier spending this time here working with you. You're amazing and a great help. I feel like I'm starting to really get this stuff. Thanks. I really appreciate it, and I appreciate you for helping me."

She thought she might throw up, but she swallowed hard again. "Thanks. Ah, okay. Our time's about up, so let's hit this next equation."

***

Test day came and Alex was as ready as he ever would be. He was confident. The tutoring lessons were over. The test was easy for Willow. And she knew Alex would do well because he knew everything that was on the test. The next day they met in the hall. He noticed her, smiled, and walked on by with two other players. *Well that's that . . . until the next time he needs help.*

She met Mary for lunch as she always did, and Mary gave Willow a look. "What's going on?"

"What? What do you mean?"

"It's all over school. You and Alex. Somebody saw you and him at the library. Mandy knows and is furious. Be careful and watch your back. She's a vicious cat."

Willow absorbed all this. She hadn't heard anything. "I was tutoring him for the calc test is all. That's it. And screw Mandy. She doesn't bother me."

"All the same. Be careful."

Mary was right. After last period Friday afternoon, when Willow was leaving school, Mandy and three of her cohorts confronted her.

"Hi, *bitch*!" Mandy started. "You keep your slutty ass away from my Alex! He's mine, you little slut! If I hear you ever even look at him again, you'll be sorry." The four of them walked by her, all of them giving her a shove or a shoulder.

Willow looked around to see who was watching the encounter and saw Alex with three of his teammates. He saw her look at him and turned to his friends, saying something. Willow turned and ran for home as fast as she could. *God. Now everybody will know I'm a loser. Mandy will make sure of that. I was so stupid to get involved with anybody, especially Alex.*

He's probably laughing about it with her right now. I was so stupid.

She got home and told her parents she wasn't feeling well, went up to her room, fell into her bed, and cried. Her mother came up a while later, knocked, and went in. She felt Willow's forehead for a fever.

"You don't have a temperature. What's wrong, honey?"

"I just don't feel well. I don't think I can eat dinner."

"Can I make you some chicken soup? You always like soup when you aren't feeling up to par."

"Maybe. Maybe later. I just want to rest."

"Did something happen to upset you?"

"No, Mom! No! I just don't feel well and want to be alone."

"All right. Okay. I'll check back later." She left.

Willow lay there, then finally got up and put on her pajamas and crawled into bed. She opened her computer and started her homework assignments, hardly able to maintain any concentration. Her mother came up about an hour later with some chicken soup, left it on her desk, and left without a word. Willow was hungrier than she thought and devoured it. She went back and worked on her homework, finding it hard to focus, with a gnawing sense of apprehension about what tomorrow would be like when she had to go back to school. She turned off her light at nine, which was standard bedtime for the whole household. She was still awake at ten and heard a plink on her window. She got up and looked out and saw Alex, dimly lit by the street light. She opened her window and with a loud whisper asked, "What are you doing here?"

"Can you come down? I need to talk to you."

"About what? Your girlfriend?"

"She's not my girlfriend anymore. Not after what I saw. Please come down. I need to talk to you."

"Shhhh. I'm coming." She shut her window, threw on some sweats and shoes and snuck quietly downstairs and out onto the porch. He was standing out by the street and she beckoned him to come up to join her. Her parents' bedroom was in the back, so they could talk quietly on the porch swing.

"What do you want?" she asked angrily. "Haven't you done enough damage? I'm ruined. I'm ashamed to go back there after today."

"I'm so sorry for what happened with Mandy. That was so wrong. She had no business doing what she did."

"Then why didn't you stop her? You were there. I saw you watching."

"I just got there at the end, when she was walking by you. I saw her give you the shoulder. Two of my friends were trying to tell me what happened and when I turned to find you, you were gone. But I did catch up with Mandy, and we're done. It was actually kind of funny, I mean, the way she threw a fit and everything. I don't really know why I ever went out with her. She's not a nice person. Deep down, I guess I always knew that. My buddies all hated her and kept warning me. But she was popular and good-looking. I wanted to tell you I'm sorry for what happened. Tell you what, I'd like to pick you up in the morning and we'll go to school together. Then let them talk."

Willow sat for a long time in silence. "But why? You don't need to do that. I'll be fine."

"If we walk in together, they'll all, I don't know . . . maybe let it all go. I already saw Mandy's tirade on social media. Didn't take her long. God, I really despise her right now. I really owe you a huge favor. I've been trying to find you all week to let you know that I aced that test. Thank you for helping me out. I owe you now, more than ever. And I want to show them all that you are my friend. You're a really nice girl and I like you."

She sat again in silence, absorbing what he had just said—especially about liking her. "I don't understand. Why would you like me? Just because I helped you out for a test? As you might recall, I sort of got into a jam about that, by offering to help you cheat."

He hung his head. "Yeah, I know. I'm apologizing about that again. It was a boneheaded idea and I handled it all wrong. But you still hung in there and we did it. And I like you because you are fun and nice. I liked having our study meetings. I looked forward to them and I miss them. You really helped me. Hey, it's late and I gotta get home or I'll be trouble. I'll pick you up tomorrow at 8:15."

"But—"

"No buts. Tomorrow at 8:15." He got up and left, turning back once to wave at her and give her a thumbs-up.

She sat thinking about all this. It was a bit much for her to wrap her head around. *He broke up with Mandy and now he wants to take me to school so we can walk in together. And he said he likes me?*

She went back to bed and her heart was racing. *I'm not sure about this.* After another restless night, morning came and she took a little more time with her hair and upped her dress code a few notches.

Her mom looked at her and commented, "You seem to be feeling better. And look at you! You certainly look nice today. Something special going on at school?"

"No, I just feel better. Must have been the chicken soup. Thanks Mom." She grabbed a slice of toast, slathered on some peanut butter, grabbed

69

her backpack, and ran out the door, hollering, "Bye, Mom! Gotta go! Alex Bancroft is giving me a ride this morning and he's waiting."

"Alex who?" But it was too late. She was already gone.

Willow got in the truck. "Alex, this is going to be really awkward and I don't think it's a good idea at all. It's bad enough kids might see me getting out of your truck."

"It'll be okay. I got you into this and I'll do what I can to get you out of it."

They got to the high school and pulled into the parking lot along with seemingly everyone else. As they exited and walked toward the front door, he took her hand. She tried to pull away, but he held on tight. A terrible thought came to her. *What if he's just setting me up. He'll take me into school and laugh at me and go back to her. That's what he's doing. I'm so stupid.*

He turned to her. "See? Not so bad."

"I can't do this, Alex."

"It'll be okay. Trust me. It'll be okay."

She took a deep breath. *I hope so. I hope so.*

They went in and started toward their lockers. Everyone stopped talking and watched them walk by, like they were a couple going to their execution. *Dead couple walking.* Then she saw Mandy. *Shit!*

Mandy stepped out in front of them and

confronted not her but Alex. "How could do this to me? With that little nobody? How dare you?"

Alex looked at her and said loud enough for everyone to hear, "A nobody? A *nobody*? Look who's talking. I've known Willow for about three weeks and she is ten times the person you are. She's nice, she's smart, she's fun, she's pretty, and she's way more interesting than you'll ever be. Out of our way." And he shoved their way around her, not without throwing some shoulder into her the way she had done to Willow the day before. By that time the hall monitor had arrived and was moving everybody along.

Willow let out a huge sigh and felt a lump rise in her throat. *I can't cry!* She swallowed it away and said to Alex, "Thanks, that was nice." She picked her head up and walked proudly to her locker. She and Alex parted to go to their respective homerooms. No one said a word about anything all day. Alex quickly took her home after last period so he could get back to basketball practice.

***

Willow was still on edge from the day and her mother noticed. "Willow, something has been going on with you. Things aren't okay, are they? Talk to me."

"Oh, Mom . . ."

"Don't *oh, Mom* me. Tell me what is going on. Are you having difficulties at school?"

"Yeah, sort of . . ." She related what had been happening the last few weeks and all she knew about Alex. When she finished the story, her mother sat quietly for a minute then smiled. "Good for you, sweetheart. It seems you have a new friend. And he sounds like a nice guy. Do you like him?"

"I guess. I've really never been interested in boys. I just thought I was destined to always be a nerd." She looked off into space, and took a breath. "Yeah, I guess I like him. He is nice. It was like he was protecting me today. And then he confronted Mandy in front of everybody. I was so embarrassed, but it felt nice."

"Well, I think you might just have a new boyfriend, like it or not. Just be careful." Willow picked up on several implications in "be careful."

***

Willow was doing her homework when she got a text on her cell phone. The only person who she ever got texts from was Mary and when she checked it, she was surprised to see it was Alex. She remembered they had exchanged phone numbers when she began tutoring him.

"Have you been on social media? It's all over.

Alex and Willow are a couple and Mandy Johnson is a loser. I'll pick you up at 8:15 tomorrow."

She sat there, stunned. *Mandy, a loser. She was nuts before, now she'll be totally crazy. And Alex and I are together.* She laughed quietly at that. *Yeah, right.*

***

Willow and Alex arrived at school and walked in together. After the last morning period, Alex found her. "My buddy Jason, who's in the same homeroom as Mandy, said she didn't show today. And he said that he's in her psych class, and she didn't show there either, and apparently they had a big test today."

"She's probably embarrassed to show her face, if what you texted last night is true."

"Didn't you see it? It was all over."

She laughed. "I don't do social media. Never have. Sounds sort of silly, posting all the stuff I hear about, like, so and so did that and I'm doing this, or here's a picture of my cat and so on. I don't have time. Rather read a book. Oops, sorry. I didn't mean to offend you."

He laughed back at her. "No offense taken. You're so different, Willow. So different from all the others. I really like you more all the time. Hey, the new Star Wars movie is in town. Would you like to go see the late afternoon show Saturday? And we can go have something to eat after."

She almost choked and swallowed hard and stammered, "Like a date? I've never been on a date before. I don't know, Alex. I don't know what to do on a date."

He looked at her incredulously. "You've never been out on a date? You're kidding. Why?"

"No one ever asked me and I wasn't really ever interested." Which was a lie. She had secretly always wanted to have a date and had been asked out a few times but the idea made her nervous and she had always declined. After those few denials, any such offers vanished. Word was out. Now here was one of the most popular guys in school asking her out. She knew him and liked him. "Sure. I'd like to."

"Great. My friend Kyle and his girlfriend are going with us, so it'll be fun. First date then, huh?"

"Yep, so be nice." She smiled up at him. "Thanks for asking. That's nice."

"It'll be fun. Kyle is funny and Cindy is really nice."

"Cindy Kelley? She was in ALP Spanish with me. She is nice. I liked her."

Alex said, "Great. It'll be fun. I really want to see that movie. Hey, gotta get to my next class. See you after last period."

***

That night she noticed how good dinner was and thanked her mom when she was helping clear the table. Her mother commented, "You're in good spirits tonight. Have a good day at school?" "Yeah, very interesting." She told her mother about her upcoming date.

Her mother smiled warmly. "I'm very happy for you, sweetheart. You know, your dad and I will need to meet him."

"Of course you will."

She texted Mary with the news and Mary was both astounded and happy for her.

Willow giggled all the while as she was doing her homework. Getting ready for bed, she just started laughing at how all this had transpired. *I have a date with one of the most popular guys at school. How ridiculous is that?* She laughed herself into a sound sleep.

THE ANCHOR

"**B**illie, set some damned anchors," I yelled up at her. She was high up on the near-vertical granite wall, much too far above her last rope anchors for the belay rope which I was holding tightly and anxiously in my leather-gloved hands.

***

Billie and I had taken rented canoes to the far end of a lake in a rugged, mountainous area of Montana to do some rock-climbing. We could have gotten by with one but she, being the independent woman she was and always determined to make her own way, had to paddle her own. I had learned over the eight months we had been together to stay out of her way when she was determined to do something.

She had heard of this place from a customer at REI in Salt Lake, where we both worked. After an early start, it had taken us the better part of the first day of our five days off to drive up to and paddle across the lake, to the landing site by the place we wanted to climb. The alternative would have been to have a helicopter take us in, but that was way beyond our budget.

We off-loaded and carried what we could to where we would set up camp. There were six other climbers already there, probably choppered in since we saw no other water craft. We exchanged pleasantries with them and found a spot to set our tent. We went back to the canoes and got out the cooler with food and beer for the next three days.

***

I had grown up outside of Santa Fe, where I roamed the desert almost as soon as I could walk. I was turned on to rock-climbing by one of my high school friends and was hooked. I earned a degree in education with a minor in literature at the University of New Mexico in Albuquerque. My goal was to be a high school teacher so I would have summers off to play in the desert and rock-climb. After graduation, I got a job teaching in Los Lunas, but resigned after two years, being disillusioned with the educational system and not quite ready to grow up. I took a road trip that summer exploring and climbing in Colorado and

Utah, eventually ending up out of money, in Salt Lake City. My outdoor experience got me a job at REI, where I met Billie.

We got to know each other and became climbing buddies on our days off. We became close friends, then lovers. She was beautiful with her close-cropped dark hair, high cheekbones, fine features, and soft hazel eyes. She was long, lithe, and an excellent rock-climber with long, strong arms and legs. She was like a spider when she climbed. Her climbing was as beautiful to watch as she was beautiful.

***

It was more and more frightening watching her do this pitch. She was now way above where she should have already set several anchors for the belay rope. Right now she was free-climbing. Even though she was wearing a harness, it would do her no good if she fell. She looked in complete control, but this was not a mapped line, where she was. Two of the other climbers joined me.

"Geez, man," one said. "She needs to set some anchors. She's way beyond her last one."

"Yeah, I've been telling her," I said, trying not to show the panic I was feeling.

***

Billie was raised in Boulder, Colorado, along with a younger sister and an older brother. Her parents were both rock-climbers and mountaineers and had all three of their children out in the mountains at an early age. Billie took to the mountains like a duck to water. She couldn't get enough. By the time she was in high school, she'd already made a name for herself among the climbers in and around the Boulder area.

She earned a certificate in Outdoor Recreation Leadership at Colorado Mountain College in Leadville, Colorado. After that she worked at the National Outdoor Leadership School out of Lander, Wyoming for a year, working with young adults. For whatever reason, she left NOLS, moved to Salt Lake and started working for REI.

Billie was one of the toughest women I had ever met. Her mornings before work were at a nearby CrossFit center. I would join her a few times a week, and she always showed me up with her strength and stamina. She thought nothing of a ten-mile run at five in the morning. Her goal, by her thirtieth birthday, was to solo Everest. She was now twenty-three. I had no doubts she could, and would, somehow manage to do it. At this moment, I was wondering if she would live that long.

***

"Billie, dammit! Set some damned anchors. You're scaring me!" I screamed up to her.

She yelled back down to me, "Shut up, Ryan. I've got this. You're making me nervous."

She reached for her next handhold. Then she stretched out her leg at an impossible angle, found purchase with her toes and swung her body another two feet upward, two feet closer to the top, or possible disaster. She had maybe ten or fifteen more feet to the summit. She now had to be over sixty feet high, her last belay anchors set maybe thirty or thirty-five feet lower.

Another climber had joined us. "Wow, she's amazing. That's a really difficult route, gotta be in the 5.12 to 5.15 range. She's gotta be one of the best climbers I've ever seen."

"Yeah, she's good, all right, but I wish to hell she'd set herself some anchors."

"Oh crap! Yeah! Oh my god. Yeah, she hasn't. That's no place to be free-climbing. That's a dangerous wall."

More panic was building in my chest. My stomach was churning. I took some deep breaths. I wanted to do something, but was helpless. It was up to her. *Dammit, Billie. Set some damned anchors.* I was wishing her to do something. Anything.

Two more of the climbers had gathered around me, watching, not saying anything. Just when it looked like she had it made, she reached her right hand up with those long arms, feeling around for a handhold, finding it . . . I could almost see her staring in disbelief as I watched her fall, as if in slow motion, useless rope coiling in the air above her. She didn't scream, but I saw the look of terror in face, even from so far away, as she clawed to find purchase, but found only air.

***

Billie and I were lovers, mostly on her terms. I was enamored with her. I really didn't know about love or what it was, I only knew I wanted to be with her. I enjoyed her energy, her enthusiasm for life, and the great, wild abandoned sex.

I wanted to move in together, but she said she needed her space. I made the point that she was either at my place or I was at hers every night. Her answer was she didn't want to commit to anything. She didn't know much longer she was going to be in Salt Lake. She didn't want to be tied down. She wanted her freedom. NOLS was asking her to come back. She was considering maybe applying for a position at

Outward Bound and several other outdoor schools. All she talked about were all the opportunities she could have here or there or somewhere else.

All our conversations were either in undertones or overtones, neither of us ever getting said what needed to be said. She would ignore my gestures of love. She was a free spirit. It was becoming clear that I was but a momentary blip on her radar. It hurt, but maybe that was my attraction to her, her remoteness to love and commitment, her focused drive to achieve her goals. Maybe I wanted to be like her and hoped what she had in her singularity and focus would rub off on me. In many ways, I was jealous of her.

***

The group around me gave an auditory gasp as they saw her begin to plunge to the rocks below, her arms flailing, trying to grab the rock.

Miraculously, her rope, coiling wildly above her, snagged an outcropping of rock after she had plummeted about twenty feet. I braced myself and two other guys, seeing the same thing, quickly grabbed ahold of me and braced themselves. The slack was snapped up a moment later, almost pulling all three of us off our feet, as we watched her fall instantly stopped. The rope had held on the outcropping. Her athleticism showed as she immediately righted herself and had her feet toward the wall to stop her as she swung toward it.

"God, I hope she's okay. That was really a hard stop," somebody muttered.

"Better than the alternative," said another.

We all were watching now, with our mouths open like gaping fools, at what we had just witnessed. Nobody said anything. Every one of us was hardly breathing. We saw her moving and grabbing purchase on the rock. Her next move was to grab an anchor off her belt and wedge it into a crack and tie off. She set another anchor and was now doubly secured, then she set a third. Stabilized, she sat there in her harness. I could see her breathing hard, wiping her eyes.

She called down in a shaky voice, "I need to check the rope and make sure it's okay." She found the downside of the rope and did a quick loop hitch in her harness to secure it. Then she untied it from her harness and pulled it over the outcropping, letting the loose end fall. She then pulled it back up and carefully examined it. "It's pretty frayed. I'm going to cut it and get rid of it," she called down.

We watched her as she found her knife and cut the frayed part off, letting it drop. She retied the rope to her harness and threaded it through her anchors. "I'm ready to come down now." With the rope safely in her anchors, I could now belay her down.

Minutes later she was on the ground and collapsed. I was first to reach her. She was on her hands and knees, crying, shaking, retching. I took her in my arms and held her for a long time as she slowly regained her composure.

The first thing she said was "How could I be so stupid? I'm sorry, so sorry. I was in the zone. I didn't want to stop. Just wanted to keep going. I thought I had it. I know better. It was a stupid, stupid, stupid, asinine thing to do. I would've died if that rope didn't catch. Just hold me for a minute. I want to feel alive. I just want to feel alive . . ."

Always in control, she had never seemed so vulnerable, like a child with a badly skinned knee. I held her gently but firmly, feeling a lump rise in my throat and tears of relief form in my own eyes. She finally stopped shaking. Then she just went limp and let me hold her.

"Okay, I think I need a beer," she muttered.

"I need more than one, plus a tequila shot or two," I said.

"You brought tequila?" That was the last thing she said.

I put away our gear while she slowly sipped on a beer. I prepped some food and we ate. One of the other campers came over and asked if we wanted to join them. I looked at Billie, who was now staring off with vacant eyes at the granite wall that almost took her life, and said, "Thanks, but I think we'll pass." He nodded his head, said good night, and left.

She said flatly, "I'd like to get out of here tomorrow. I'm finished." She said no more.

"Understood. We can pack up and head back early, then."

She said nothing more, never looking at me. We crawled into the tent and sleeping bags. She turned away from me and feigned sleep. Her night was fitful. She woke me several times, calling out, "No! No! I can't. No! I don't want to die. I want to be alive. I can't do this anymore. I'm sorry, Daddy. I don't want to. Mommy, Mommy, I'm scared."

We were up at dawn. She helped pack up like a robot or a zombie, with mechanical movements and no words. Gear and supplies loaded in the canoes, we headed back across the lake. There was a blankness about her. She was empty, her eyes vacant, like all energy—like her very soul—had been drained from her. Like there was nothing left.

When we landed, she went to the van and sat still, staring, maybe in her mind at that granite wall. I returned the canoes to the rental place, loaded our gear in my van, and headed down the deserted highway bordered by dark, foreboding hills. She had lost herself. And I was losing myself as I wondered for her survival and my love for her. We drove on into a gathering storm of thunder and lightning, where her dreams would never be the same.

KATIE

It was on a farm outside the little town of Hope, Iowa, about fifty miles south of Des Moines, where I spent my childhood. I once had a friend there by the name of Katie Evers.

My dog, Skipper, and I would wander off here and there to explore and see what we could see, find what we could find. My dad, a hired man, and at times my mother, worried I was lost, and sometimes spent hours looking for me and Skipper. We'd most likely be in the woods half a mile away from our farmhouse, or hiding in the hay mow, in a cornfield, or sometimes in the orchard next to the chicken house, generally with me reading a book. Skipper and I always knew where we were. We were right where we were and never lost.

Once when I was ten years old, Skipper and I ventured over a ridge where my folks had forbidden me to ever go—which was all the better reason to go over that ridge to see why we were forbidden to go there. After about a mile, we went down a hill and happened upon an old cabin at the edge of a wood of old Iowa hardwood trees.

The cabin looked old but in good repair. It was surrounded by flowers and had a large fenced garden next to it. An older-model pickup sat in a weather-beaten shed. Birds filled the trees, singing upon our arrival. Skipper and I decided we should turn around and leave, but we heard a woman's voice. "Hey, what are you doin' around here? You lost?"

I looked around and saw a woman standing in the door, and answered, "No ma'am. We aren't lost. We're right here."

She looked pretty tough and sturdy, dressed like a man, with black pants, a blue denim work shirt, and heavy boots. She had really short hair for a woman.

She laughed. "Good answer. Would ya like some cookies and lemonade? It's pretty hot out. Ya must be thirsty from your journey."

I hesitated, but answered, "Yes ma'am. That'd be really nice." Skipper and I approached warily.

"Come on in, then. What's your name? And who's this little guy?" she asked.

"This is Skipper and I'm Johnny Dalton, from over there." I pointed toward the farm.

"I'm Katie. Katie Evers, from right here. Grab a chair."

Her cozy cabin was dark, lit by only two small windows. When my eyes adjusted to the dimness, I saw dried plants hanging everywhere. The room was spotless and it smelled wonderful, like all the flowers of spring and the hay and alfalfa and straw and oats of summer, the incense at church, and anything else that smelled fresh and warm and good. I also smelled fresh-baked cookies from the plate sitting on the table. She poured me a glass of lemonade and placed two cookies on a plate which she set in front of me. I greedily bit into one and wonderfully sweet taste filled my mouth. The lemonade, both bitter and sweet, filled my mouth with a zest that made my taste buds come alive.

Katie was pleasant and friendly, asking me all about who I was, where I lived, what I liked and did. When I was finished with my cookies and lemonade, I got up and said, "I best be getting home, or they'll think I'm lost again and come lookin' for me. It was nice to meet you. Thank you for the cookies and lemonade."

"Come back anytime, Johnny Dalton. I'm always here."

Skipper and I did go back quite a few times that summer. We went over on Saturdays after I started school in the fall. One day I told some of my school friends about Katie. They looked at me like I had instantly become some sort of pariah.

"Crazy Katie? She's a witch and eats kids, ya know. Probably fattening you up for her winter eats," one said and everyone laughed and jeered.

"She's not a witch. She's nice and I like her. We're friends."

"She's probably making you into a witch too. You gonna eat kids like she does?"

They all laughed at me. Embarrassed and angry, I walked away. From then on, the kids I thought were my friends either teased me or stayed away from me. But there was a girl, Samantha (who went by Sam), in my class who would still talk to me. We became the brunt of schoolyard jokes and more teasing.

Even though she was a girl, she was really nice and fun to hang around with. She lived about a mile away from me and we would ride our bikes to each other's houses on Saturdays to play and do homework. One Saturday I asked her to go to Katie's with me. She hesitated. "I don't know. Will it be okay?"

"It'll be okay. She's really nice. I go over there every once in a while. She always has cookies."

We trekked on over to Katie's place and she greeted us at the door. "Hi Johnny. Good to see you. Who's your friend?"

I introduced Sam and we were invited in for cookies and lemonade. Sam was very quiet, like she was afraid of her, like she was the witch she was rumored to be. Katie and I chatted on like normal people, and eventually Sam included herself.

Sam asked, "What do you do with all these flowers and things you have everywhere?"

Katie replied, "I'm an herbalist. I dry these plants. Some I grow and others I harvest in the woods. Then I make tinctures to take to Des Moines to sell."

"What's an herbalist and what's a tincture?" Sam asked.

"Well, many plants and flowers have natural healing qualities. Our ancestors knew all about how to use them to create healing potions and ointments. I'm just carrying on the tradition that I learned from my grandmother, and she learned from hers, and so on, back quite a ways."

Then Sam said straight up, "Folks around here think you're witch and eat babies. I don't think you're a witch. You seem really nice and make really good cookies."

Katie didn't respond immediately, but turned away, looking beyond us, out a window. After some long moments of silence, Sam said, "Did I say something bad? I'm sorry."

"No, sweetie, you didn't. I know what people think of me here'bouts. Those rumors started right after I bought this cabin and thirty acres and moved in. I'm not married. I don't go to any of the churches in town. I live by myself in this old cabin. I try to be friendly, invited folks to come by, but nobody ever did, and nobody ever talks to me. I'd go into Hope and people'd stare at me and I could hear 'em whispering after I'd passed. I'd go into a store and folks would move away from me. I don't understand why somebody started such vicious gossip about me. I'm not a witch. I try to make things to help folks, to help them heal and feel better. I went to a few places in town to see if they'd stock my tinctures, but they laughed at me, told me to get out. So now I gotta drive my old truck fifty miles to Des Moines where I've got some stores that sell my stuff, and I do pretty well. I have my mortgage paid off and can pay my bills. I love my little paradise here. It makes me really sad to have everyone talking behind my back." She wiped her eyes with the back of her hands.

Sam and I just sat there, not knowing what to say. I piped up, "We know you're not a witch. You're really a nice lady and I'm proud to be your friend."

"You're my friend too, and I won't tell my folks I came by. Promise," Sam said bravely.

Katie stared at us for a minute, and her eyes narrowed and a shadow fell over her face. "Do your folks know you're here?"

Neither of us answered. We just hung our heads

and looked at our empty plates, and shook our heads no.

"You better skedaddle then, and don't come back til your folks say it's okay. They'd love an excuse to try to run me out, and you being here without your folks' knowin' is all they'd need. They'd run me out of Hope, for sure. Now, git."

Both wide-eyed at the outburst, we quickly left, running most all the way home. We were out of breath when my mother met us at the door. She had been watching us and saw where we were coming from. She did not look happy.

"Where have you two been? I've been calling for you for the last half hour." Her voice echoed the frown on her face.

I stammered and then said much too defensively, "Over there." I pointed off to the north of Katie's place. "We weren't doing anything, just lookin' around."

"That's not where I saw you comin' from. You're comin' from over there." She pointed directly to Katie's. "Don't you lie to me, young man," she said angrily. Then, more kindly but still coldly, she said, "Sam, you best go home now."

Sam looked at me, turned, ran to her bike and was gone in a flash. I knew I was in trouble.

"You were at that witch's place, weren't you? You tell me, now, 'cause you know I'll find out."

I knew she somehow would find out, so I said, "Yes ma'am. We were at Katie's." Then I said, more bravely than I felt, "She's really nice. She's not a witch. She gave us cookies and lemonade."

"You go to your room, mister, and stay there. You had cookies, huh? Well you won't be needin' supper, then. Now, git."

I slunk off to my room. Skipper followed me, snuggling next to me as I lay down on my bed and cried. I hadn't cried in a long time, but I did. I cried and cried. Katie was nice woman. She was my friend. She wasn't a witch.

I was grounded forever. I was hardly allowed to leave the house. I wasn't allowed to ride my bike or see Sam. I wasn't allowed to go roaming. It was like I was in prison. It was school and home. I still saw Sam at school, but we never got to go to each other's houses anymore.

School never was much fun, but I liked learning and I was pretty smart. But other than Sam, I had no friends. I read a lot of books, mainly novels I checked out of our small-town library. I must have read most of what they had there by the time I went to high school.

***

I didn't go back to Katie's until I was a senior in high school. I thought about her a lot and always felt bad for disappearing from her life like I did. One Saturday morning that spring, I told my mother I needed the pickup to go to the library, but as I was going by, at the last minute, I turned off and went down the lane to Katie's cabin. I was nervous and scared at how she might react after so many years, but I needed to let her know why I never came back.

I was greeted by a large dog who barked at my arrival and then came over with tail wagging, looking for some petting and attention. Katie was in the garden and came to the gate to see what the dog was going on about. I was standing next to the truck, petting my slobbering new friend. I smiled and said "Hi."

She acted startled until she recognized me. A broad smile came over her face and she said, "Well, I'll be. Johnny Dalton. Looks like that ol' mutt likes ya. We never get visitors, so you're the first. Gracious' sakes, you growed like two feet since I seen ya last. Come on in and tell me how yer doin'. What's it been? Three, four years?"

"More like eight. I'm a senior in high school now, graduating next month and off to college in the fall." Then I blurted out, "I'm really sorry I never came back to see you for so long. After that last time I was here, my parents found out and grounded me forever. And then, well . . . No excuses. I'm really sorry. I missed you. How've you been?"

"I missed you too, Johnny, but it's okay. I understand and ain't holdin' no grudges. Anyways, I'm doing good. Gettin' along but slowin' down a bit. Ain't no spring chicken anymore, ya know," she said with a forced laugh.

There was gray in her still short-cropped hair and more wrinkles on her face. Her eyes had lost some of their luster and looked more sad. Her features seemed even more hardened.

We sat and talked for over an hour, with cookies and lemonade, of course. She was thrilled to see me and have someone to talk to. It was like we picked up right where we had left off from eight years ago.

"I promise I'll be back more often now. If you ever need any help around here or with anything this summer, I'd be happy to do any chores you might need."

"Thank you, Johnny. That's mighty nice of you. I'll keep that in mind. Always somethin' to do round here, ya know."

"I'll be back whenever I can get away. It was great to see you again."

"Good to see you too, Johnny Dalton. Ya'll come back anytime, but be careful you don't get grounded again."

"Don't you worry." I laughed. "I think my parents are beyond worrying if you'll eat me or not."

That summer, and the following summers and holidays while I was at the University of Iowa, I always managed to get over to see her. Sometimes I'd help her with odd jobs or harvesting plants from the woods. Other times, we'd just sit and talk.

***

Sam and I had continued our childhood friendship. It eventually turned into being high school sweethearts, and then into lovers who were now contemplating marriage. We had moved in with each other our junior year at the University of Iowa, where she was studying for a degree in physical therapy.

After we graduated, we moved to Des Moines, where I found a job in a bookstore and Sam had no trouble finding work in her new profession. My college degree was in literature and creative writing. I wanted to be a writer, so working around books all day was like being in heaven. Of course, my parents thought it was ridiculous to study to be a writer. "What good are writers?" they would always say.

I, and sometimes Sam, would go down to see my parents and Katie whenever I had time. However, working full-time and writing short stories to create a portfolio that I hoped would get me into the Iowa Writer's Workshop, my trips south were only every one or two months.

A year later, one Saturday in early spring, as I was leaving Katie's, she stood, looked me straight in the eyes and said, "Johnny, you're like the son I never had." Then, for the first time ever, she took me in her arms and gave me a long hug. She then held me at arm's length and looked at me for a few moments and said in a husky voice, "Goodbye, Johnny Dalton. I've been lucky to know ya and have ya as a friend." I noticed a wetness in her eyes and left feeling disoriented, a lump in my throat, wiping tears from my own eyes.

A week later on Sunday afternoon, I got a call from my mother. She told me that a neighbor had spotted smoke over by Katie's place and went to see what it was from. He saw her cabin engulfed in flames. He rushed to his house to call the Hope fire department, then hurried back to see if there was anything he could do. He saw her truck in the shed, so he ran around trying to find her. The flames were so intense he couldn't get close enough to the cabin see if she was inside. By the time the fire department got there, there wasn't much left to it except smoldering ash and embers. After they got the fire cooled down enough, they searched for her remains. They found them in the area where the kitchen had been.

Mom said, "Dad and I know you've been over seeing her for quite sometime. We're very sorry."

"Thanks for calling," was all I could say and I clicked off, collapsing into a chair in shock. I don't know how long I sat there, thinking of Katie and our times together, our talks, her cookies and lemonade, the sweet scent in her cabin from her herbs. I especially thought of the last time I saw her and how she'd said goodbye. I heard the door as Sam came in from work.

"Johnny, what's wrong?" she asked. "You look like you lost your best friend."

I responded with a hollow voice, "It's Katie."

"Oh no! Did something bad happen?"

I told her what I knew, shaking my head from side to side as though that might change things, knowing it wouldn't, couldn't. I'd never see her again. Emptiness rolled over me. I was realizing for the first time how important she had been to me.

"I'm so sorry. That makes me really sad. I'm sorry I had to work the last time and wasn't able to go down with you. I was so wanting to go down to see her."

Sam made us each a strong drink and we reminisced over all our times we'd had with Katie, talking about her life which was so rich and full of wisdom, but how sad and lonely it really was. We talked about the stories she told of growing up in the Ozarks in southern Missouri, about how she was descended from an indentured slave from England, who after serving his time, moved west to the Appalachians, later descendants moving farther and farther west, eventually ending up in the Ozarks. She told of how her women ancestors had the wisdom of the healing power of herbs and how the knowledge was passed on from generation to generation. How sometimes, instead of healers, they were considered to be witches and were shunned like Katie, or worse.

After a fitful night's sleep, I called the funeral home in Hope asking them if they would get her remains so there could be a proper burial. The man I talked to laughed and told me they'd have nothing to do with that witch. I told him what I thought of him and his narrow-minded town and hung up.

I called a funeral home in Des Moines. They agreed to make the arrangements and do the necessary paperwork to get permission for her to be buried on her farm. Since it was an unattended death, her remains needed to be looked at by the state medical examiner to determine cause of death. It took two weeks, but all they could ever determine was that she'd perished in the fire.

I knew of no family so I wrote what I knew about her in a short obituary for the Des Moines paper. A week later I had a call from an attorney, wanting to set up an appointment. When we met three days later, I found out she had left a will and I was both executer and sole beneficiary of her farm and a small sum she had in the bank, plus a few stocks and bonds. She had written that I was the only person in the world who she loved and trusted and, I in turn, had been a loyal and kind friend. Stunned, I signed some papers and left. He had given me a key to a safety deposit box where I found the stock and bond certificates, which had some value, an album of old pictures, I guessed of family, and some old jewelry. She had made her will only two months previously.

On a Sunday morning later that spring, Sam and I buried Katie Evers' ashes on an east-facing hillside on the farm she had so loved. We got a small granite marker that read, "Here lies Katie Evers. She was a loyal friend, herbalist, and baker of great cookies." Sam and I were married next to her grave a year later.

A Bottle of Dope
and Shine

I t was 1967, and I was returning to the naval Seabee
base in Gulfport, Mississippi, from two weeks'
leave in Iowa visiting my family. I had been stationed
there for a little over a year and had made the trip
twice before. Being a low-paid enlisted man, I would
drive the 950 miles straight through, since I didn't
have extra money to spend on a motel.

I was somewhere in northern Mississippi. It was
pouring rain and the bugs on my windshield had
smeared into a greasy film that my tired eyes could
barely see through.

This was before the Interstate System had made it
south, so I had to drive two-lane roads through every
little town along the way. It was slow going, and I
had been on the road for about sixteen hours and was
ready to be back on the base and in bed. I had maybe
two or three more hours to go.

Needing gas and barely being able to see the road with the downpour and smeared bug grease, I spied a sad, lonely gas station with its lights on. I pulled into the gravel drive and up to the pump. The attendant came out to top off my tank. He was a grizzled old man with a bushy white beard, wearing a blue farm jacket over bib overalls and a greasy baseball cap.

I told him to fill it and went into the station, across a sagging porch and through creaking screen door, noticing the old, gray, unpainted, and rotting wood siding. The floor inside was bare wooden planks. The counter was made of two twelve-inch planks with a barrel at each end. The ancient cash register was open with its drawer looking like a ragged old tongue. The walls were bare wood. An old red ice chest in one corner was filled with Coca Cola.

There were several other men of equal disposition sitting on wooden folding chairs around a card table, where a game was in progress, all drinking Coca Cola. The game was halted and all conversation stopped as they all turned to stare at me like some foreigner— that, I most certainly was in that part of the country.

While I shuffled around waiting for the attendant to come back in so I could pay, I noticed them passing around a fruit jar, topping off their bottles of Coke. It was clear liquid in an unlabeled fruit jar and I could only guess that it was moonshine. Some of my buddies and I knew where we could get fruit jars of 'shine, illegal corn liquor, from a guy back in the woods north of Gulfport. We would get some to take when we went camping for the weekend over on the Pensacola beach. What I can say about the 'shine we got was that it went down smooth as molasses but kicked like a mule. I learned to be very careful of it because I would be a babbling idiot after only a few drinks.

***

One of the old boys asked, in one of those thick southern drawls us Yankee boys could barely decipher, where I was headed. I told him I was in the navy and heading back to the base in Gulfport. They all nodded their heads in approval. One smiled a toothless grin that made me feel a bit more at ease.

The attendant came back in and I asked if there was anything I could do to clean the bug slime from my windshield. They all looked at me like I was some sort of ignorant fool.

The biggest, ugliest of them all, the one with the toothless grin, said, "Son, get yourself a bottle of dope and run your wipers. Then pour that dope on and it'll clean 'er right up. Works every time." Everyone nodded in agreement.

Dope? What is dope? I thought. The look of ignorance on my face must have been obvious because he added, "Coke, son. Get a bottle of that Coke outta that chest over there. It'll clean that windshield right up proper."

One of the others added, "Best darn cleaner you can find. So do you want a little shot of this corn likker to drink on the way, young feller?" He offered me the jar.

"Thanks, but I've been driving since four this morning and I have to be back for muster tomorrow, so I'd better pass. But thanks. Appreciate the offer."

"Awe, come on, son. Just a nip. Do ya good for those last miles. Have one for god and country. You're servin' your country for us and we want to show ya a little appreciation."

I didn't want to insult these folks and was afraid if I refused I would, so I nodded and bought two bottles of Coke, one for the windshield and one to have a nip of their shine. They all smiled their approval after I took a pull from my Coke and offered it to be topped off. The man smiled up at me and filled my bottle. I thanked them, said goodbye, and walked out the door swigging my Coke and 'shine. It was really good. I started the wipers and poured the other bottle on the windshield. It worked. The glass became crystal clear.

I got in my car and headed down the road with

a clear windshield and a bottle of likker-laced Coke. The rain had stopped. The Coke and 'shine perked me up. As I drank, I thought about how well the Coke cleaned the windshield and considered what that must do to a person's stomach. I arrived back at the base safe and sound in good time for a few hours of needed sleep before 06h00 reveille.

I learned later, originally, Coca Cola was laced with cocaine and in the Deep South, folks still called it *dope* despite the fact cocaine had been illegal for years and was not used in the drink anymore.

However, experiencing how well Coke would clean a windshield of bugs like it did, I never drank another Coke again.

STARLIGHT

"Sorry," he said to the dusty, worn out midnight parking lot.

No moon. Only the stars lighting the desert surrounds with cold emotion. Dry cool air tonight in the desert outside the unpainted worn-out bar with the single neon sign that read simply Earl's. Five troubled, sagging pickups in a row, worn-out seats covered with Navajo blankets and sheepskin.

Melancholy music from a worn-out, over the hill, hippy band reflected through the thin walls and was swallowed into the darkness.

Matt choked down a sob and again exclaimed, "Sorry," to no one. A coyote sang an eerie song, sounding like a banshee from another time.

He walked into the darkness at the edge of the lot to piss out the beers and tequila shots he had been drinking since sunset, embracing that lonely time when he wouldn't sleep again. He walked to his old BMW motorcycle, mounted, cranked it, and sped from the parking lot, pitching gravel to the four directions. He accelerated to a hundred, a hundred and twenty, then a hundred and thirty miles per hour, the bike rock solid and steady between his legs.

Maybe tonight I can do it. I want to do it. I want to end the pain.

He was almost outrunning his headlight beam, looking for something to slam into. But there was nothing. Only endless desert, a straight highway to nowhere and soft sand, dirt, small rocks, cactus, sage, and scrub all around. No place to adequately end it. He knew that already, after six months of going down the same road almost every night. Overdosing on pills had seemed like a good way, but he couldn't do that either. Maybe he should move closer to a major highway and head-on a semi.

Shit. Face it, asshole, you just don't know what you want. Don't want to live; don't have the guts to die, he thought.

He finally slowed and turned up the dirt road to his old trailer house. *Fuck,* he thought. *Another wasted night. Another with no sleep in sight, as always. Fuck, fuck, fuck! I just want to sleep, just want to sleep . . . just want to sleep.*

***

108

Matt was the typical golden boy, straight As, captain of the high school football team, handsome at six feet and a hundred and eight-five pounds, with his gray eyes and shock of blond hair. He gave up numerous academic and athletic scholarships and joined the army two weeks after high school graduation. He excelled as a soldier, easily went up through the ranks to sergeant. Three tours in Afghanistan, wounded his last tour. Now discharged and broken.

He lived in an old two-bedroom trailer on ten acres of desert that he had taken ownership of about a year ago by paying five years' worth of back taxes. The property tax was only a hundred dollars a year. It was about five miles from a small northern New Mexico town and only four miles from Earl's on the outskirts. Once he had chased out all the mice, snakes, and other assorted critters, plugged numerous critter holes, and cleaned it up, it was home. The appliances still worked and he liked being away from humanity but close to the roadhouse tavern.

It was a little after midnight when he turned into his short drive. He saw a small, dark figure walking down the road. *Interesting*, he thought, *this time of night*. He pulled in and parked his bike.

He was opening his trailer door when he heard a female voice say, "Hey, hello? Do you have some water? Please? I am really thirsty."

He turned, looked, and replied, "Well, yeah . . . Sure. I can get you some. You got a water bottle or something?"

"Yeah."

"Come on over and I'll go in and get you some. You okay?"

"Yeah . . . Fine, just really thirsty and really tired. Been on the road since early this morning."

He took her water bottle, went inside, and turned on the lights. He filled it and took it back out to her. He then first saw her from the porch light on the trailer. He guessed her to be twenty-something. She was dressed like some sort of gypsy waif in a long, colorful skirt and a down jacket with a pack on her back. *She sorta has a glow about her*, he thought. *Beautiful. She could be an angel.*

"Thanks," she said, and started to drink it down like no tomorrow.

"Whoa! Slow down girl," he said. "You'll cramp up, drinkin' so fast."

She paused, smiled. "Thanks. Ran out around seven tonight. Thought I'd find someplace before now."

"Not much around here, especially this time of night. You're still a good five miles from town," he replied. "That's a long time in the desert without water . . . You're lucky. Where're ya headed?"

"Headed? Nowhere in particular. Just down the

road. Guess I found out the hard way how deserted and dangerous the desert can be. Thanks for the water. Could I have a refill?"

He took her jug and went inside and filled it and when he turned, she was right there in front of him with her big smile. In the light, he really saw this beautiful tanned woman with a wide smile, wild, curly dark hair and turquoise eyes flecked with gold. She took the bottle and drank some more.

"Hey, would you mind if I crash outside by your trailer? I'm exhausted. Beyond tired. More like close to dead."

Not really, he thought, but feeling sorry for her, he said, "Sure, yeah, you can crash here, but not outside. Stay inside. Use the couch. The bathroom's over there. Help yourself to whatever might be in the fridge. It probably ain't much, but it is what it is . . . It's home."

He found an old blanket and a towel for her.

"This is the best I got. I'm going to bed."

"This is great. Thanks so much. You're a godsend."

That night he slept the best that he had in at least a year. *Strange*, he thought when he awoke in the morning feeling almost rested. He shambled out toward the bathroom, in his birthday suit.

"My, my," he heard a female voice say.

"Oh shit, shit, shit." He'd forgotten all about

her being there and ran back into the bedroom, embarrassed all over.

Clothed, he shamefacedly came back out to a smiling face.

"That was nice," she said, giggling. "Not bad, not bad at all."

"Yeah, right. Sorry."

Then he smelled the eggs, the toast, and the coffee she had prepared. Suddenly hungry, he was amazed that he actually had food. Then he remembered that he had been in town a few days ago and had stocked up on a few things. Happy now that he had. She bade him sit, and she served him up and sat across from him, and they began to eat. He was hungry. Interesting, since he never ate breakfast. He really didn't eat much at all. They ate in silence.

Finished, she gathered the dishes and took them to the sink. She came back and poured more coffee.

"Sleep well?" she asked.

"Yeah, I did. And you?"

"Slept well, thanks. Your couch was way better than hard ground. Mind if I use your shower?"

"Please, go right ahead. There's never much hot water. Actually, not much water at all, so be quick. Please. The cistern doesn't get refilled until tomorrow."

He was always almost out by delivery day, under normal circumstances. *Hell, she'll be gone today.*

No problem.

She gathered her pack and went in. He heard the water start, then in a few minutes, stop. *Thank you,* he thought.

"Wow, that felt so good. Did it cold, just to cool down from the last few days on the road. Got the major grime off, I think. Thank you so much. You're a great guy."

"No problem," he muttered.

"What's your name?"

"Matt, Matt Calandar. And yours?"

"Cheyenne, just Cheyenne." She looked at him with her big eyes and smiled. "So why are you trying to kill yourself?" she asked.

"What? What the fuck . . . What the fuck do you mean?"

"Sorry, I'm sorry. I see things and know things. Sometimes things I probably shouldn't know. I'm sorry. I shouldn't have, but you seem like such a nice guy. I want to help you if I can. I like to help people."

"Aw shit, woman, I mean, Cheyenne, I'm way beyond help or redemption. I've tried it all: fucking VA, fucking counselors, fucking psychiatrists, fucking all of it. I still have the fucking dreams . . . Can't sleep. I drink too much. I can't be around people—that's why I fucking live out here by myself. I am of no fucking use to myself or anyone else. I would be better fucking off dead."

And he fell back into the old armchair with its broken springs, staring out a window into space, not believing his outburst. He never ever let that happen. Never . . . ever.

She sat down on the arm of the chair and put an arm around him and held him and stroked his head. With a soothing voice, she said, "It's all right. After your three tours in Afghanistan, what you saw and what you did, I understand, but not really. I can't imagine. Let me help."

"How the hell do you know that? You don't know me. You don't know anything about me. There's nothing you can do. Nothing. I can't undo what happened. I want to, but I can't undo what I did. I can't be any more sorry. I can't. And what the hell kind of name is 'Cheyenne' anyway? Fuck, nothing about you makes any sense. Just what the hell are you doing here? What the hell do you want from me?"

"I told you, I see things. I know things and I want to help you. And I can help you, if you let me."

"Yeah, whatever. Knock yourself out. Fuck everything."

And he got up and stormed into his bedroom, collapsed into his bed, already back asleep. He slept the rest of the day, woke up enough to pee, and went back to bed and slept until morning.

He woke to smells of coffee, toast, bacon, and eggs. He shambled out into the kitchen, clothed. "Bacon? I know I didn't have bacon. Where did the bacon come from? More of your magic, or whatever it is that you do? Sorry about yesterday."

"I took your Beemer into town and got some stuff," she said. "Also called the water guy for more deliveries since there are now two of us. He came out earlier this morning so we have a full cistern. Nice bike, by the way, and apology accepted. No problem."

"We? What the hell's with this 'we' thing?"

"Well, I'm here and including you, that make two or a 'we,' I guess," she replied with a little laugh.

He liked her laugh, like a tinkling sort of music.

"Ah, excuse me. Correct me if I am wrong, but I don't recall inviting you to stay for more than one night. Last night makes two. Ever think you might be overstaying your welcome?"

"Naaaah, I know when my time somewhere is up and always move on by my own accord," she said, smiling another little laugh. "It isn't time for me to leave yet. I would like to hang around for a while. It'll give me a chance to explore the desert, something I haven't had a chance to do yet. Please? I will stay out of your way. You won't even know that I'm even around. And I cook."

He considered this. *She does make a mean breakfast,*

and I've actually slept. There's something about her that I feel good about. Maybe it'll be all right for a while.

"Okay, you can hang out for a while, but I reserve the right to kick you out if and when I want."

"Deal."

And so began a sort of strange relationship. She cooked him breakfast and then would disappear for hours in the desert, or borrow his Beemer to go into town for groceries and supplies, which she always had money to help pay for. One way or another, she would be home for dinner, which Matt had now started to cook. The only times he really saw her were at breakfast and dinner. She would sit and smile while eating, telling him about all the things she'd discovered in the desert or what was happening in town. She would show him some stones or bones she'd come across that interested her. After they finished, she would always ask how he was doing and if he wanted to talk.

Same answer: "Fine and no."

This went on for about three weeks. Matt became curious, wanting to know more about her. He was beginning to like her. He tried asking her some basic questions about herself, all of which she would always evade. He asked her where she was from. "Here and there." Did she have family? "Not really." Did she go to college? "For a while." Where? "Not important."

How old was she?" Old enough." What do you want from me? "Nothing, really." And so it went. She remained an enigma.

Cheyenne continued to appear quietly and mysteriously from nowhere. After a few weeks, he was getting used to it and was less and less startled by her sometimes immediate presence in his peripheral vision or being right behind him when he would turn around.

One day Matt decided to follow her on one of her desert sorties. After she left, he waited, then started trailing her, carefully staying out of sight. She walked for maybe less than a quarter of a mile to a grove of piñons which she disappeared into. The piñons backed up against a high rock cliff along the side of a hill. A moment later she reappeared and hollered for Matt to come in and join her.

Shit, I should've known that she'd know. She fucking knows everything. "Okay, all right, you caught me."

He reluctantly walked toward her, afraid of what she might want. She reached to him, took his hand, and led him into an alcove under a rock overhang. A 'shrine' was the only word he could think of to describe it. There were some animal bones, some stones placed in specific configurations that he didn't understand. There were several bundles of sage, which gave a wonderful perfume to the space. And a blanket that was placed back against the rock cliff in front of which two very large crystals stood upright. She drew him into the alcove and sat him down on the blanket with the larger crystal right in front of him. She dropped down beside him, facing the other crystal.

"Welcome to my sacred space. I've been expecting you," she said, smiling up at him. "I come here every day to meditate and recharge myself. This is the most wonderful retreat I've ever had."

He felt something in his solar plexus, a warm, comforting feeling, the likes of which he couldn't remember ever feeling before. A strange peace settled over him and he decided that he might like to stay there forever.

"Nice, huh?" she said.

"Uh, yeah, sure," was all he could muster up to say as he felt a lump form in his throat and tears well up in his eyes. He just sat and relished his emotion, not really understanding what it was he was feeling.

She reached over and took his hand, and they sat together in silence for a long time, several hours maybe. Time wasn't working very well for Matt right then.

Finally, she stirred and said quietly, "Matt, it's time to go."

He stirred, opened his eyes, took a moment to

get his bearings, and stood on rubbery legs. She came to him and gave him a nice big hug.

"Time to go," she said again, moving toward the entrance.

He just stood there, confused and bewildered by everything that just happened, especially the unexpected hug that felt like an electric current shooting up his spine. He didn't want to leave. She reached back in and took his hand and led him out and back to the trailer in silence.

***

Matt was sleeping consistently better and better, even without the marijuana he used frequently as a sedative. The screaming awake, dripping in cold sweat episodes were becoming less and less frequent. He was feeling good, rested, had more energy, was eating better and more regularly. He considered that he might actually be happy. But he felt apprehensive. He couldn't understand why he was in the place bordering happiness. He was afraid it might not last.

"Good morning," she said the next day. "What's goin' on? Happy to be feeling better, getting some good sleep, and thinking that you might be starting to be happy?"

He was about to say "What the—" when she held

up her hand and said, "Sorry. I know I'm precocious and should be less direct, but sometimes things just come out, know what I mean?"

"Yeah, I seem to be finding that out. So, what was with yesterday when we were in your grotto or whatever it is?"

"I guess I found a pretty high energy place, don't you think? You seemed to enjoy it."

"It was all right, I guess. Made me feel sort of strange. It was a good kind of strange. Yeah, I liked it a lot. More than a lot. I felt quiet and light and at peace, like when I was a kid, ya know. Something I haven't felt in, like, forever. I would like to go back again, if that would be okay. So, what is it with you? You arrive here, and I'm feeling better and happier that I have in a long, long time. Please give me a little insight. Could I go back there again?"

"Sure, you can go there anytime you want. I don't have to be there. Just go whenever you want. Come again with me, for sure. I enjoyed having you there with me. And, okay, yeah, I probably need to explain little. It will sound weird to you, I know. I have sort of a 'gift' or something, and I have found that I can use it to help people. Like you, for example. People who are suffering. I try to help them by bringing some positive vibes into their lives. I try not to impose, just hang out and be me. You seem to be happier."

"Well, yeah. I have to admit, for whatever reason, your being here or whatever, yeah. I seem to have lost some of my craziness, and I want to continue to feel halfway sane again. I don't want to go back to that place where I was when you arrived. You're right. I wanted to off myself. I couldn't stand living but didn't want to die. I was crazy, drinking too much, not eating. I was pretty nuts. I'm starting to see more clearly. It's like the fog seems to be lifting."

He was feeling comfortable and more open with her than anyone since he was discharged from the army.

"Want to keep this talk going?"

"Oh shit, no. Not really."

But for the first time, he felt that maybe he could. He felt at ease with her. Something was happening deep down that made him want to unload to this strange woman. *Now would be the time, if ever. Time to get it over with,* he thought.

He took a deep breath and tensed.

"I don't know if I can. I could never share it with any of my therapy whizzkids who didn't really give a shit because they were so overworked and stressed out from all the other crazies in the VA hospital. I finally just up and walked out, one day. Couldn't stand it. It was making me more crazy, being in that loony bin."

"I'm here and I'll listen. No judgment. I'll just

listen. Come on, open it up. Get rid of it."

Matt sat back on the couch and began to stare blankly out of the window. His breathing became very shallow and heart rate became more rapid. He started to talk in a low monotone voice.

"It was on my last tour in Afghanistan. My team was returning from a patrol. It was a long day. We were tired, thirsty. Ran out of water. We were humping by a little village and there was a woman out doing laundry, her kids playing in the dirt. I stopped and asked if she had any water. She smiled and nodded and proceeded to fill our water bottles. We returned to base.

"A week later we went by the same village and I stopped by the same house to give the family some food to say thank you for her kindness. I went in and what I saw——" He choked back a sob. "They were all dead. Heads chopped off, the mother and the little kids. All naked and decapitated. The bastards found out. The fucking bastard heathen barbarians wanted to send a message and they cut off their heads. It was my fault. I knew I shouldn't have done it. Never should have stopped. I knew better. It was my fault. It was my fault, it was all my fault. And I know that is why I got shot . . . My punishment."

He ended in a small, weak voice, still staring blankly out the window, hardly blinking, just staring, his breathing slow, still shallow. He was in a cold sweat, his shirt soaked, breathing, breathing, breathing. He closed his eyes and fell asleep. His breathing became regular and deep.

She covered him with a blanket, sat beside him on the couch, pulled him over so his head rested on her lap, and sat with him all night long, whispering in his ear, "It's okay. It wasn't your fault," over and over and over again.

He awoke in the morning to the wonderful smell of breakfast cooking. She was working her magic at the stove with bacon, eggs, and pancakes. Pancakes?

"Good morning. How're ya doin'?" she asked.

He took several deep breaths. "All right, I think. I seem to feel lighter or something."

"Do you remember what all you told me last night?"

"I remember you talking to me and asking me to open up. I remember I started telling you about what happened in Afghanistan. What all did I tell you?"

"I think pretty much everything. At least, stuff that I think really mattered. I think unloading all that stuff, whether conscious or not, was something you needed to do. And you need to realize, what happened was not your fault, as much as you seem to want to accept all the responsibility. It's too big a burden. You do not need to carry it any further. Let. It. Go."

"Don't know if I can."

"You already have. Trust me, you already have."

She continued by asking about him being shot. He replied that he took two bullets his left thigh, shattering the femur. It was a messy process getting his leg back together again without having to amputate it.

"I spent a year in rehab and can now walk without a noticeable limp. I took a medical discharge and that's why I'm still on disability."

Without a word, she came over, sat beside him, and placed her hands on his left thigh. He felt something shift, not quite sure what it was, but the annoying minor throbbing pain he kept experiencing seemed to disappear.

Just don't ask, he thought to himself.

Breakfast was ready and they sat and savored it. Afterward they went outside to drink their coffee and enjoy the clear desert morning.

***

They hung out together for several months. She taught him a meditation practice that she called 'angelic meditation.' They spent time together in the shelter meditating, roaming the desert, walking, talking. Matt was bordering on happy, even ecstatic. He felt like something was no longer present. Something big and dark had gone away. He was seeing more clearly. He was loving the solitude of the desert and seeing the nearby mountains, smelling the sage, watching desert critters do their thing, seeing it all seemingly for the first time. So much he hadn't noticed for such a long time. He hadn't had any alcohol in over six weeks.

And then there was Cheyenne. What was it with her? He couldn't figure out his feelings for her. She was a beautiful woman—kind, caring, warm, comforting, loving, made a great breakfast—everything he could want in a woman for a possible serious relationship. She was so much more than any other woman he had known. He didn't really understand love, but he thought he might be in love with her, or just love her. But strangely, he didn't feel any physical attraction toward her, which he couldn't understand. It was almost like what he felt for his sister or mother, but it was still a different feeling that he could not explain or understand. Whatever it was, it was a powerful emotion.

One night Cheyenne seemed strangely uneasy and restless. After dinner she began fussing around, trying to be busy doing nothing. Finally, she announced that she was going to the grove and wanted to be by herself. She needed to be alone to do some meditation for guidance, or something.

Matt inquired if he could do anything to help, to which she replied firmly, "No!"

He said no more and let her go do her thing.

Feeling a little anxious, he decided to roll a joint—something he hadn't done in quite a while. He got out his stash, went outside, sat down, and went about his business.

"Ahhhhhh." Feeling mellow, he was enjoying the moonless, cool brightness of the beautiful, starlit night. He was staring out into the desert, enjoying the darkness that seemed to penetrate his very being, when he thought he saw a golden glow of sorts moving through the desert.

"What the hell? The Mary Jo?" he said to himself as he blinked, trying to focus. Yeah, there was definitely something out there, a glowing something, and it was coming closer. This was getting weird. Very weird. He sat watching it come closer. Then it faded into the desert darkness. And he heard her voice.

"Matt, is that you? Are you outside?"

"Yeah, what's going on? I am a little stoned and I thought I saw some sort of glowing apparition or something. It was freakin' me out. Marijuana never did that to me before. Then you appear out of the dark. What the hell's going on?"

"Sorry, Matt. Didn't mean to startle you. But we

need to talk."

Those 'we need to talk' words were words he didn't like to hear. Reminded him too much of all his ex-girlfriends who used those very words right before the breakup. And they were the favorite words of the stupid therapist. "Matt, we need to talk." The outcome was never good.

She came and sat down in front of him, took his hands in hers, and said, "It's time for me to move on. I have to go. I like being here with you. You are a nice guy and I like being around you. But I need to go now. You don't need me anymore, and it's time."

"But . . . but . . . What the hell?" he stammered. "Leaving? Why? Where're you going? I like having you around. You've taught me and shown me so much about a lot of things. I haven't felt this good in years. I really don't want you to leave. Whoever you are, having you around is good for me. I need you here. I don't want you to go. Please stay. I think I'm in love with you."

"You aren't in love with me. You'll be fine without me. You don't need me anymore. You're whole again. Trust me, I know. I'll certainly look you up when I return this way, but it's really time for me to leave. I'm sorry, but I do need to go. Now!"

She was emphatic and he realized that he couldn't stop her. She was a woman of her own mind, as he well knew by now. One of the few things he did know about her. He knew she wouldn't change her mind. And like that, she went inside, had her pack loaded, gave him a peck on the cheek and a hug, and was gone into the night, toward the road.

He heard a car stop and a door slam and then speed off. *Strange. There're never any cars on the road this time of night. And she walks down to the road and one appears? What the hell? Nothing makes sense anymore.* Between the marijuana-induced haze and the events of the night, he was totally confused. So he did the only logical thing at that point: he rolled another joint and tried to pretend that he hadn't seen and experienced what he just had. But it was all real. His experience was definitely real. And she was gone.

He lay back on the ground and contemplated the starry night. Millions of bright lights, so far away. He awoke the next morning, still on the ground, shivering from the desert cold.

The realization dropped on him like a load of rocks. She had left. She was gone. His world suddenly seemed empty, like a part of him had left with her.

The next few weeks, Matt felt tired and listless. He poked around the desert, did his meditation practice. He missed her. When he visited the grove for the first time, he noticed that the big crystals had disappeared. The stones and bones were also gone. Nothing remained except for the blanket and some sage.

"Interesting," he thought. "It's all gone. She's gone. I'm alone again."

It was like he had imagined the last months, and that it was all a dream. But the fact that he felt somehow human again was proof that something had happened. But what? Who was that woman? What the hell happened?

Nothing was the same. After several weeks of moping around, he discovered that he was lonely and wanted to be around other people. *But definitely not the dregs at Earl's. Not anymore.* They were like the walking dead, burned out old druggies, Vietnam vets, washed up and sad old men. He wanted to be around healthy human beings. And he did not drink anymore, maybe a beer once in while, was all. His need to get drunk was gone.

He was sleeping. His dreams were pleasant. No screaming, cold-sweat nightmares of hacked-up bodies. He was eating, making his own breakfast, having lunch, and going into town about every night for dinner at a local café. He was eating healthy. He was sort of amazed at himself and how good he felt.

His leg felt great and he started running again, short distance at first, then longer runs through the desert after his morning meditation.

Once he got over Cheyenne being gone, he found he had more time available. He started reading and was making trips to the bookstore and coffee shop in town every two weeks or so. He became a good book-buying customer.

He found he liked hanging out at the coffee shop, meeting some of the locals and talking with them—small talk about the ever-changing weather, what was going on in town, who was who, and so on. He started to feel a connection with the community.

Two years later

Matt was straightening out the books and magazines in his bookstore, newsstand, and coffee shop which he had purchased several months before. It was four o'clock and his night clerk would soon be in.

Some weeks earlier, when doing the same thing, a book had fallen off the shelf. He had just straightened it and then it just fell off. It was a titled *Angels Among Us*. It looked interesting, so he took it with him and began reading as he sat behind the cash register. He couldn't put it down and read it in one long, late night. Some of the stories in the book reminded him of his time with Cheyenne and that whole episode of his life came rushing back. It all started to make sense. Sort of.

Nah, no way. It couldn't be. She couldn't have been. That's just plain silly. Weird, he said to himself.

That night, Matt had a dream in which Cheyenne appeared. She was like golden sun, like whatever he saw that night in the desert before she left. She was smiling at him with her beautiful smile. He kept reaching out for her, but she receded into the distance until she finally faded away and then there was nothing except a glowing crystal. It was all he could remember the next day, just her dream presence as a golden glow. She seemed so real. She seemed close.

He rose early and went out to the grotto to meditate, as was his daily routine. Upon entering the alcove, he noticed a small crystal had somehow appeared overnight in the exact same place where she would always sit. He stared at it for several minutes. He detected a hint of gold shining deep within.

What the hell? Unbelievable! Totally fucking unbelievable! Maybe she really was . . . Nah! No way! Quit thinkin' that weird shit!

***

Matt was straightening the magazines when a young woman came in. She disappeared into the New Age section. After about fifteen minutes, she came to the register to buy a book about the healing and metaphysical properties of gems and stones, along with the local newspaper.

"Hi," she said, flashing a beautiful, broad smile. "My name is Angela. Angela Morris. Do you know of any places for rent? I'm planning to relocate here. Some folks in Santa Fe told me that I should check it out. I've been casing it for a few days and I like it here. Nice town. Nice energy."

She continued rambling on without hardly a breath. "I grew up in Iowa and spent the last seven years, since graduating from Iowa State, working in Minneapolis and I'm sick of Midwest winters. I want moderate and dry. Winters are just too brutal up there. I'm tired of living inside eighty percent of the year because it's so freakin' hot or freakin' cold."

"I'm a computer software developer," she went on. "I have three patents and am working on my next. I like that I'll be able to work from here and never have to be in an office in a thirty below zero blizzard ever again."

She caught herself. "Sorry, I tend to ramble on incessantly when I get nervous, and I'm nervous right now because you look so familiar, like I should know you. But haven't a clue. Please, help me out. Have we met before? You look so familiar, like . . . like where have we met? When?"

Matt just stood there, dumbfounded, staring

at this beautiful tanned woman with wild curly dark hair, and turquoise eyes flecked with gold. *Unbelievable,* he thought. *She looks just like her. It can't be.* He remembered her saying the night she left, "I will certainly look you up when I get back this way."

"Hey, are you all right?" Angela asked.

A lump had formed in his throat and tears were welling up. He managed to choke out "Excuse me a minute" as he quickly went into the back room.

There, he leaned over the sandwich prep counter with both hands, his eyes rolled upward, inwardly gleeful. *You did say you would be back. You just keep messing with me, don't you? Thanks. Thanks big time. I thought I was in love with you. Now I know for sure,* he thought to himself.

Regaining his composure, he returned to face Angela Morris. Smiling, he lied and said, "Sorry, I have allergies and needed my inhaler. But when I see you, you also remind me of someone, someone I knew a while back, but I don't think we've ever met before. Long story. I'll tell you sometime. I'm happy to meet you, Angela Morris.

"And, by the way, my name is Matt, Matt Calandar. I own this place, and interestingly, I have a nice apartment over the bookstore that has become recently available. Reasonable rent. All updated.

Cozy. Comfy. Nicely furnished, with Wi-Fi. Want to take a look? My night guy's coming in a few minutes and I'd be happy to show it to you, if you think you might be interested. We can check it out, see what you think. Maybe we could catch a bite afterward?"

"Hey Matt, good to meet you. Yeah, I'd love to have a look and, yeah, I am starved. Is this a first date?" she asked with a flirtatious smile, a smile he knew so well.

"I suppose it could be," he said with a goofy grin.

Nick, the night guy walked in. "Hey, Matt! I'm here. Anything I need to know?"

"Nope, it's all yours. Have a good night. See ya tomorrow."

Matt took Angela's hand. "Let's go look at your new digs."

"Yeah," she said, squeezing his hand, looking up at him with a warm smile. "I love new beginnings."

SWINGING ON A STAR

"*Swinging on a Star*" by Bing Crosby was my mother's favorite song. Those old, forgotten lyrics came sneaking back into my head as I sat on the hill down below the old farmhouse where I grew up so many years ago. I remembered how she would hum the melody or sometimes sing the lyrics when she thought no one was listening, while she cooked, did laundry, gardened, and did all the other chores around the house and farm to keep my father and the hired man fed and in clean clothes. But that was a long time ago.

Dusk was settling in after a normal, hot, sultry July day in northeast Iowa. No breeze to ruffle even the lightest of leaves. Frogs were singing down in the valley by the spring-fed farm pond. Mosquitos hadn't yet come out or else hadn't found me yet. A humid mist rose from the valley floor. It was an evening that brought back those childhood memories from what some might call the 'good times.' But only remembering the good times means we have put the bad times away.

Now were sad times. I had buried my mother that morning. Dad preceded her by six years. She was a tough one, eighty-nine years old, only just going downhill in the last few months. She had a good life. As an only child born late in her life, I now had to consider the eight-hundred-acre farm I had just inherited. Right now the old farmhouse was filled with friends and neighbors finishing off the day with casseroles and Jell-O salads.

I was leaning against the old oak tree where my long rotted-away swing had once hung from a high branch. My dad made the swing for me, a single twenty-foot piece of hay rope with a wooden two-by-four for a seat. I loved to come up here and swing. There was a flat spot on the hill, near where the tree stood. I would walk up to where the hill again began to ascend toward our house, straddle the rope and, with my legs straight out so I wouldn't hit the ground, sail out into space like I was flying. With only the one rope in the center, I went backward and sideways and spun in space. It made me feel alive and free, like I could do anything: have adventures like Peter Pan, Tom Sawyer, Captain Ahab or Ishmael, or the western heroes of Zane Grey's many books.

However, my adult life turned out to be less

than adventurous. Now an account executive with an advertising agency where I coddled and sold advertising to untrusting businessmen and women—who never seemed to be satisfied with the outcome of any ad campaigns the agency ran for them, no matter how successful they were—I was good at what I did. I made decent money, had a nice condo overlooking a park in Cedar Rapids which I bought after losing the house to my ex-wife. She and her new husband lived there now with our two kids, both now in high school, who I got to see one awkward weekend a month. Ten years and I hadn't found anyone to be serious about, mainly because I wasn't really looking.

I brought my mind back to the present, settling back into the woodland sounds and smells. A train whistled about a mile away going up along the Mississippi, the big engines working hard. I remembered hearing those trains through my open bedroom windows during the summers before we had air conditioning. How they always made me feel lonely, like I needed to be somewhere or going there, maybe somewhere out west where the purple sage and wide open spaces of Zane Grey novels were.

I used to love these days and nights of soft summer air, always wanting them to go on forever. No school, just freedom. Free run of eight hundred acres, about a third in hilly woodlands with the remaining hilltops in crops. I would roam through the woods, climb the bluffs, sometimes finding arrow heads and other treasures, now all packed away in the attic of the farmhouse along with all my other old things that my mother kept.

After supper some nights, I would come down and play on the swing. One night, I remembered, a particularly bright moon rose. I was on my swing going so high I thought if I let go at just the right time I might fly all the way through space and time and land on the moon like the astronauts did fifteen years earlier, in 1969. Maybe higher. Maybe even to the stars.

A female voice jolted me back to the present. "Travis, your guests are getting ready to leave. You might want to go back up to the house and say goodbyes."

I turned to the voice and saw Molly Ann Parker standing in the shadows. Molly Ann and I grew up together. Her parents' farm was close-by and we'd play together on Saturdays during the school year and roam the woods together during the summers. We were inseparable until freshman year in high school, when she decided she didn't want to hang out with me anymore. She found new friends and she began avoiding me. Lost and alone, I finally started hanging out with some guys from school. Then in junior year, my best friend Carl started dating her. After that, he wasn't my best friend anymore. They ended up getting married right after high school because Molly Ann was pregnant.

After college, I relocated to Cedar Rapids, about a hundred and twenty-five miles away. I came back to the farm frequently, especially after Dad died, then more in the last six months with Mom's failing health. I only ever went to the farm, never socializing in town. Most folks never knew I was there, especially Molly Ann, who I purposely avoided. I hadn't seen or talked to her in twenty-five years.

Molly Ann was right. I needed to get back to the house. There were still guests and I needed to thank them all for coming. All the women from my mother's church had brought food—so much food it could have fed a small army.

As we started up the hill, she asked, "How are you holding up?"

I stammered, "Uh, okay, I guess."

"I'm very sorry about your mother, Travis. I truly am. I lost both my parents some years ago. I can understand what you must be going through. You're lucky to have had your mother this long."

"Yeah, I suppose I am. I don't know if it's really sunk in yet."

"It takes time."

"Yeah, I suppose it does. I really should get back up there and say goodbyes." I started to walk faster.

She kept right with me. "I'd like to stay after and talk awhile, if that'd be okay?"

Again, I stammered, "Uh, yeah. Talk? Sure. Of course."

We walked the rest of the way in silence, me wondering what we'd have to talk about. Where was her husband?

After shaking everybody's hands and again accepting their sympathies, the house was cleared of everyone except for Molly Ann. We were alone and I was fidgeting, uncomfortable, being with her.

"It's good to see you, Travis. You look great."

"Thanks. You're looking good, yourself," I answered all too sharply. "How's Carl?"

"I don't know how he is. Carl left me two years after we got married. I haven't seen or heard from him since our divorce."

It took me a moment to process what she'd said, and I muttered half-heartedly, "Ah, I'm sorry, Molly. Really. I've been through it myself and can sympathize. Sucks."

She waited for more from me, then continued nervously, as though needing to fill the emptiness, the distance between us, with sound. "Yeah. He couldn't handle the responsibilities of fatherhood and moved on, leaving me alone with the baby. My parents helped me go to junior college and become a medical assistant. So, I was a single mom and now my daughter, Emily, is a senior at Iowa State, trying to get into veterinarian school."

She paused and, me failing to respond, she continued, her voice beginning to quiver. "I've thought about you a lot, Travis. I'm sorry for treating you like I did, you know. Like I did back then. I've wanted to see you for a long time, but you fell off the radar. I knew you came here a lot to visit, but you were never around. I'm sorry this circumstance was what finally gave me the chance to see you."

I grunted a response, not feeling much like hashing out old stuff. I looked by her, not wanting to meet her eyes.

She continued, "It was wrong of me, I know. Just all of a sudden, I don't know, just to ignore you like I did. It was stupid. But I wanted to explore, to have girlfriends and check out other guys. We were always so close. I needed space. I should've talked to you then. I shouldn't have just cut you off like I did. But I was young and didn't know how to talk to you about the things I felt. I'm sorry. I know I must have hurt you."

I grunted again, not having any response. The anger and confusion I felt back then came rushing back. She didn't say anything, just stood there.

Then, with dripping sarcasm in my voice, I said, "I'm sorry. I don't know what to say. Seeing you after all these years, the way things happened back then. You really did hurt me. Just all of a sudden, you ignored me, like I was a pariah or something. I thought we were friends. But no. You went off made other friends. Never talked to me. You were popular. I was just another kid. Maybe it was my fault that I never really had any really close friends in high school. I don't know. But I hated it."

After several long moments, I looked over and saw her standing limply with her hands at her sides, her palms turned toward me as if pleading. She had tears running down her cheeks.

Seeing her just then took me back in time to when we were maybe twelve. I remembered her pleading with me over some most likely inconsequential thing. I remembered the fondness we had for each other. The anger, hurt, and regret faded away like the morning mist in fresh sunlight and tears wanted to swell my eyes too. I did something crazy. Something I had wanted to do back when we were kids. I went to her, took her in my arms, raised her chin gently, and kissed her with all the pent-up passion and love for her I didn't know I had been carrying with me for more than twenty-five years. I felt her body stiffen for a moment and then relax. Her arms went around my neck and she responded to my kiss with the same passion.

We took a breath. She whispered, "I've always loved you, Travis. I had to grow up before I realized it. By then you were gone. I've longed for this moment, not thinking it would ever happen, to hold you close, to kiss you, to feel your warmth."

I was savoring her, wanting her, desiring her. I heard the night sounds coming through the screen door. The crickets seemed louder. More frogs had joined the chorus. Somewhere close-by an owl hooted.

I whispered back, "I don't want to ever lose you again. Don't go away from me again. We have so much we need to talk about. We need to get to know one another again."

She turned her head back to me and leaned back from my arms still holding her tight around her waist, and looked me in the eye. Tears were running freely down her cheeks—from fear, sadness, or happiness, I didn't know.

She began talking rapidly, immediate. "Are you sure? If we're starting something, you won't easily get rid of me. This has to be for the long haul. But we both have baggage. It's been a long time. We both have different lives now. It could get very complicated.

I don't want to hurt you. Or get hurt."

My mind was racing. I placed my finger gently on her lips. "Hey, slow down, already. It could be complicated, okay. It could be very complicated. But I don't think we're starting something new. I'd like to think we're continuing something we started long ago and never totally realized 'til now. Now we can spend time catching up, getting to know one another again.

"I've got a lot to do here, sorting out the farm and estate, so I'm going to have to be here a lot. We can see how the next few weeks or months go. Get to know each other again? My options are open right now. I have some ideas for what I want to do with the farm and it will all take time. I'm planning on being here for at least the next few weeks, for sure, and maybe full-time when I get the farm up and running the way I want."

We were quiet for a while, each absorbing what was happening, still not letting go. She was the first to break her hold, wiping her tears on her sleeve. Looking and smiling at me, she said, "Can we take a walk down by the old tree where the swing was, where I found you earlier? Remember the fun we had with that swing? It's a beautiful night with a full moon. I wish that swing was still there."

I replied, "Sure, I'd like that. I wish it was still

there too. Then we could pretend we were swinging on a star like we used to."

"We can still pretend we are, anyway. I think I already am." She took my hand and pulled me in for another kiss.

BECKY AND RICHARD

"I'm tired of trying to see the good in people," said Becky.

She was having iced coffee with her friend Richard. They were sitting on the patio on Main Avenue where they could watch and make fun of the gawky tourists. Both were on break from their jobs, Becky a sales expert in the marijuana industry, and Richard a software developer for a tech firm in Denver.

Richard had moved to Durango during the COVID-19 pandemic, since he was able to work remotely. There, he and Becky had met and become lovers. Both were in their late twenties and liked the small mountain town ambience.

"What do you mean? Another one of your asshole stoner customers?" asked Richard.

"No, I'm used to them. It's my dad. He's being jerk again. He never lets up. He called again last night, wanting me to come back and work in his fucking car dealership. He was just awful. Called me an ungrateful bitch. My own dad called me a bitch!"

"Why does he do that? Haven't you told him you don't want to move back to Des Moines? You've certainly told me, like, a thousand times."

"Oh yeah. I've told him at least that many times, but he doesn't get it. He somehow thinks I owe it to him to carry on the family business. My brothers bailed. Did he call them bitches? No. He blessed them and sent them on to their own lives. But me? He's always demanded way more of me than my brothers. It was always, 'Excel in sports. Excel in school. You're not trying hard enough.' And my lazy-ass brothers sat around playing fucking video games all day long."

"What about your mother? What does she think?"

"My mother? Ha. As I've told you, she doesn't think unless it has to do with tennis or golf. Or she's always too busy with some fundraiser or has had too many gin and tonics to know what is going on. Talking about this makes me want to cry."

"Maybe your father just wanted you to do great things. Wanted you to do something other than work in a weed dispensary."

Becky's eyes narrowed. "Who the hell's side are you on? I like my job. I like living here. I like the people here. I don't need or want my father's overblown expectations."

147

"But when was the last time you took a brush to canvas? You have a master of fine arts in painting. And you're working in a pot shop?"

Becky diverted her gaze. "Hey, check out that couple. Total tourists. Both wearing T-shirts emblazoned with some 5K run from their hometown. They come out here looking for something special, but can't leave their hometown. Weird."

"You're changing the subject. Answer my question. Why aren't you painting?"

"It takes time. I have no time. I'm tired after my shift at the dispensary and just want to kick back when I get home."

"So quit your job."

"I can't afford to. I have bills and it's expensive to live here."

"You always wanted to move down to New Mexico and that art commune that would love to have you. It'd be way less expensive and you could focus on your art."

"I can't."

"Why?"

Becky paused a minute and wiped a tear. "I'm scared. I'm afraid of failure. What if I'm no good?"

"Dammit, Becky, you told me you earned several major awards when you were finishing your MFA. You were the golden girl, destined for greatness. All your pieces in your MFA thesis show sold . . . and for some pretty good prices. At least, that's what you told me."

"What if that's the best I'll ever do? I can't fail."

"Ah, so who's that talking? You or your father?"

Becky paused again. More tears were coming. "I don't know what to do. I really do want to paint. I have so many ideas. When I say I like to 'kick back,' I'm really sitting doing sketches. I have books of sketches ready to go to canvas. I can't afford it. I need to live."

"You told me your grandfather left you a big inheritance. What about that?"

"I'm saving it. I might need it someday. If I ever leave here, like for New Mexico, you'd be here. I'd be there. What about us?"

Now Richard paused. "Becky, what if I came with you? What if we were together down there? I've worked remotely ever since COVID. There is a home office, but only for a few of the company executives. They've given up all the rest of the office space. So I doubt I'll ever have to return to Denver. I'll go with you."

"What are you saying, Richard? You want to live together?"

"We pretty much are already. I've said how many times that it's stupid for us to pay two rents. I want to live with you. You are the most important thing in my life. I love you."

Becky checked her watch. "Hey, I need to get back to work." With that, she got up, picking up her coffee mug to return it inside.

As she came back out, Richard said, "But, Becky, I—"

"See ya soon," she said, walking by him back to the dispensary, on a sunny southwest Colorado afternoon.

THE ULTIMATE ZOOM

Max slowly awakened from his dreamless, lonely night to face yet another uneventful, long, and solitary hot, August day in Santa Fe. He yawned and stretched his limbs. He jerked his right hand back in shock when it touched another body.

***

It was now the third year of the COVID-19 pandemic. The death toll in the US was now over four million and rising every hour of every day. All foreign borders, including Mexico and Canada, had been closed to US citizens for two years. Medical science had been working overtime to find a solution to the ongoing pandemic but so far, any new vaccines had proven to be ineffective. Countries which had quickly implemented strict directives early in the fall of 2020 to wear masks, practice social distancing, restrict any and all social gatherings—and in some cases executing complete lockdowns—were the only places having lower infection rates.

After the 2020 election in the U. S., even with the new administration working overtime to curtail the epidemic, it was proving to be too late. The virus had gotten completely out of control early in the winter 0f 2020–2021 and now seemed impossible to contain.

Some state governments were doing their best to implement the federal directives, but others still refused. Regrettably, the virus was still not being taken seriously by a certain portion of the populace who, in spite of everything, still thought their own freedoms trumped social responsibility. They thought that the severity of the virus was a hoax and it would someday magically disappear.

The economy was suffering. The federal government had no more borrowing capacity to meet its obligations. There was no more aid to the unemployed. Insurance companies had discontinued all health care coverage. Overloaded hospitals were going broke. Many parts of the country, especially large eastern cities, were now in chaos, with the food chain falling apart. It was becoming completely undependable with grocery store shelves more empty than full. Many cities had to impose martial law.

Ever-increasing caseloads were leading hospitals to

set up satellites in high schools or colleges—anywhere with large, usable spaces. Proper safety equipment was almost nonexistent, as were ventilators and necessary medications. The number of health care personnel was dwindling, due to the attrition rate of those who were burned out or feared for the safety of themselves and their families. Many who had contracted the virus had no medical care at all and were left on their own to either recover or die.

New Mexico, where Max lived, had been in complete lockdown for over two years which required him to be confined to his historic one-bedroom adobe. He was only able to go out for an allocated time once a week to shop for groceries and other necessities. He was allowed time outdoors once a day for exercise, sun, and fresh air. Max, like so many others, was becoming more and more depressed, wondering if this would be the end of human life on the planet. One friend had committed suicide. Max had thought about it, but still felt he had much to live for.

With most all business now being conducted remotely by computer, which demanded better and faster interaction time, Max was still employed as a software developer and was working from home. He was thirty years old and had had no other human interaction for months beyond the biweekly Zoom meetings with his work team.

Starved for any social connection, and as a last resort, he had put his profile on a dating app. He'd had several responses. One in particular stood out: Heidi Carlson, a massage therapist from Taos. Max found her attractive with her curly red hair and freckles. She was smart, interesting, and fun to talk with. All that and a big, beautiful smile which lit up her big green eyes.

She found Max, with his deep brown eyes and poorly self-trimmed shock of wavy brown hair, "dreamy," as she had texted her best friend, Suzanne.

Max's company provided him with unlimited time on Zoom, so he and Heidi were able to spend hours together on the platform, talking and getting to know each other. The weeks passed, and despite having never physically met, they were beginning to fall in love. Their conversations were becoming more and more intimate with expressions of desire and longing for one another driving them both crazy. They were both mentally and sexually frustrated and had no idea if and when they'd ever fulfill their desires, given the present state of the world.

One night, Max, in a wildly romantic mood, said, "I just want to jump into my computer and have Zoom transfer me into your bed so we could make love. I want you so much."

"That'd be wonderful," cooed Heidi. "We could Zoom back and forth every night and spend all our nights together. Maybe if we wish really, really hard?" She giggled. "Wanna try? Bet I can wish harder."

"Sure, bet's on," said Max. "Let's wish really hard." They both laughed at the idea.

But nevertheless, wish they did, with all their hearts.

***

The warm flesh stirred and a soft purr came from the pile of curly red hair on the pillow next to him. The warm flesh now stretched and moved, the head of red hair turning toward him, eyes popping open. "What the hell? Who the hell are you? What are you doing in my bed?"

Max's eyes widened. "Your bed? This is my bed. Who're you?" Then he saw. "Heidi? What? What're you doing here? How?"

She stared at him. "Max?" Then she looked around. "Where am I? How'd I get here? What's going on?"

"How *did* you get here? In *my* bed?"

"I don't know. I went to bed last night right after we were online." She looked over and saw his open laptop. "I really, really wished I could be here with you, but . . . No, no, not possible. Ridiculous."

"What's ridiculous?"

"That I came through your open laptop." She started to laugh.

He looked at the open laptop. "Oh. I never disconnected from the Zoom link. No matter. Come here." She slid across the bed into his embrace.

After an hour of insatiable lovemaking, they finally came up for air. Heidi excused herself to go to the bathroom. Max went to the kitchen to put on some coffee and get them some toast and juice. On his way out, he closed his open laptop, setting it on the desk by the kiva fireplace. When he returned he called out to her. No response. He went to the bathroom door and knocked. "Are you okay in there?" No answer. He peeked in. The room was empty. He knew she had been there. Her nightgown still lay in a heap on the floor where it had been tossed, but she was nowhere to be found.

He sat down on the edge of the bed, feeling a little vertiginous and nauseous. His head was spinning. Nothing was making sense. It was like there had been some sort of time warp, some unknown portal through which she had traveled. She had been there. Now she had suddenly disappeared. They had physically made love. He could still feel her, smell her, hear her. He tried to focus, but his vision was blurred, and he became aware of the pressure in his brain and his rapid heart rate. He took some deep breaths to calm down.

He found his phone and called her. She answered in an instant. "Max! What's going on? I thought I had this erotic dream. I dreamed I was with you and we made love. It was so real. Then I realized it was real. I was naked and didn't have my nightgown. And then, well, then my body confirmed what happened was real. It wasn't a dream. What the hell's happening?"

"I don't know, but your nightgown is right here. You were here. I know you were. God, Heidi, I went to the kitchen to make us some toast when you went into the bathroom. I came back and you'd disappeared."

Then he glanced at his closed laptop and a thought crossed his mind. "Did you have your laptop in your bedroom last night? Did you close it?"

She hesitated a minute. "No, I just closed it now. Come to think of it, I don't think I disconnected from the Zoom link either."

They both went quiet for a long minute, then simultaneously said, "No. That can't be possible."

Heidi said, "Open your laptop and I'll open mine. Then let's wish again to be together like we did last night. Wish really, really hard again and see what happens."

"You're kidding me. I know you somehow snuck

over here and then snuck out. Why?"

"Like yeah, right. I came all the way down from Taos in my nightgown and went home naked. I don't think so! My car was repossessed a month ago, so maybe I stole a car and drove those seventy miles to your place and back, like in an instant? Really? Come on. Let's at least give it a try."

"Okay, okay. Zoom is a neat program, but I don't think it has the capacity to transport bodies like in Star Trek. Like, 'beam me over to Max's house, Zoom.'"

"Then you just fucking explain it, smartass."

"I'm sorry I was sarcastic, but this is all crazy."

"Then humor me. Let's try my suggestion. What can go wrong? So it doesn't work. You said you meditate. Then let's meditate together with a focus on this. Okay?"

"Fine," he said. "Let's at least try."

"Okay, but let me get dressed first. I don't want to travel naked through some weird continuum. Give me a moment."

"Yeah, I'd better get dressed too."

Five minutes later, each sat in front of their respective laptops. Max had sent her a link. They were connected. They both closed their eyes and began to meditate. Time passed. Max was in a state between awake and dozing. He opened his eyes and saw he was sitting next to Heidi, who was still quietly meditating.

Holy crap. This seriously cannot be happening, he thought.

He barely whispered, "Heidi? Heidi. I think I'm here."

She blinked awake. "Oh my god! It worked! It really worked!" She got up and gave him a big hug. "It has to be something to do with the theory of quantum mechanics."

"Mechanics? What are you talking about? Mechanics? Like with physics?"

"Yes, silly. Physics, particle physics, about how we observe the subatomic world which can be particles or light depending on the observer, how particles can be known to interact across space and time. Basically, it comes down to the fact that everything, us included, is made up of atoms which are made up of subatomic particles. We are all simply energy. What we observe as being solid is really all light waves or particles. So, theoretically, there's no reason our bodies, made up of light energy, couldn't simply transfer across time or space, or apparently the internet, as energy. It's all hard to explain and I don't think I'm doing a very good job of it."

Max just stared at her for a long time while she was searching for a better explanation. He said, "What the hell are you talking about? How do you know this shit?"

"I'm sorry. I'm embarrassed I never told you. I was working on my PhD in physics up until two years ago."

"But you said you were a massage therapist."

"I know, I know. I went to massage school right out of high school, then put myself through college. Okay, I'm smart. Really smart. I graduated from college magna cum laude in three years, then began graduate studies at Stanford. I was working on my PhD dissertation when I crashed mentally and emotionally. I needed a break, so I quit and moved to Taos, and set up my massage practice, now closed because of the pandemic. I'm flat broke and living in this old motel room by the week and about to be evicted."

Max looked around, stunned at the shabby room she was living in.

"Okay, if what you say is true, then there's no reason you couldn't come to my place and stay permanently. I have enough income for both of us. Pack what you need and I'll hang on to it when you close your computer and maybe, if all this works like you think, I'll end up back at my place with your stuff. Then we can do this again with you coming to my place. Put your computer on your lap and maybe everything will transmit. What do you think?"

She thought for a moment. "It's worth a try. So far, this has worked. Let's." She retrieved a tattered suitcase and threw her few belongings in.

He sat and put the suitcase on his lap. She closed the laptop and, right before her eyes, he seemed to fade into a gaseous state of light and then . . . he was gone.

Fucking amazing. It's all true, she thought. *Schrödinger was right.*

A half an hour later, she appeared in Max's living room holding tightly to her laptop.

She said, "Now let's carefully close the link absolutely simultaneously. Let's not take any chances."

The link was broken. They jumped into each other's arms and hugged for a long time. He noticed she was crying, "Are you okay?"

"More than okay. These are tears of pure joy. Kiss me."

***

A year later, the epidemic was beginning to be brought under control with people starting to realize that protective measures truly did work. Everyone had begun to pay attention and they were becoming more socially responsible by wearing masks and maintaining a respectable distance when in public. A new vaccine had been developed and was proving effective.

Heidi and Max were happily settled into a life together in their apartment, close to Stanford University, where Heidi had resumed her doctoral pursuit.

Max was still working remotely in software development. He had Zoom meetings with his team at least twice a week, making doubly sure to cut the link after any such meeting. Couldn't be too safe.

Heidi was following up their experience with new research and a totally new dissertation, entitled "Transference of Matter Through Time, Space, and the Internet." She was basing it on the fact that she, Max, and her possessions had traveled through time and space and they had replicated it four times. So far, her new research was looking promising. The government was seriously interested with this discovery and the implications for national security. Becky was working closely with them on further development. Also, CERN scientists in Switzerland had heard of her research and were interested with her discoveries and all their possibilities. They had invited her to come and discuss her findings and also wanted her to participate in the next experiment with the Large Hadron Collider in two months' time.

She was able to get permission from the government and accepted, seriously considering which mode of travel she would use—normal air travel or Zoom.

DANA'S STORY

I stepped out of my little adobe house into the bright blue sky of morning, feeling a little hungover from Suzanne and me partying a little more than we should have last night. I stopped by the French Bakery in an alley off the plaza for a chocolate croissant and a cup of their decadently rich coffee. I sat at one of the sidewalk tables and thought of my day and the new case I was working on, the letter and all of yesterday's drama already forgotten.

CHAPTER I

All I can say is that I had an unusual childhood. My parents were super uptight conservative types, my father a big executive at a downtown publishing firm and my mother a wannabe tennis pro and gin and tonic queen. She tried to play her dutiful role as a homemaker, but that consisted mostly of telling our housekeeper what needed to be done for the day.

My father would come home from work at precisely 5:30 every evening. Mother had his cocktail and the newspaper ready for him. There were no words spoken, no questions or comments on the day. Dinner was also spent mostly in silence, other than "Please pass the potatoes."

I truly believe the only time my parents might have ever had sex was when they spawned me. After I arrived, they figured one was enough. I think they considered me more like a pet, like a dog or cat, than an actual human being. Something their friends could ooh and ahh over. Give me some treats and put me back into my cage, or I should say, my room. In our case, children should be neither seen nor heard.

It was not what I would necessarily call child abuse, as in many ways, it was easier for me.

Kindergarten was a shock to me. Seeing there were others like me. Little girls and boys. What were boys? Needless to say, my social skills weren't. I spent my recess time hiding and class time trying to hide.

As the years progressed, school was spent studying, getting good grades, and not much else . . . No sports, no extracurricular activities, and no social life. I managed to make friends with two girls who were just like me—bookworms, none of us at all popular. Boys were an enigma. The only ones we could hang out with were ourselves.

At the end of my senior year in high school, much to my surprise, a guy asked me to the senior prom. He wasn't one of the popular guys, for sure—not very good-looking, tall, skinny, with acne and unruly red hair. I was hesitant but reluctantly agreed to go with him. My mother was surprisingly thrilled and took me shopping for a dress, shoes, and a new hairstyle, different from my usual boring ponytail. When I got dressed the night of the prom, I looked in the mirror and was amazed that I actually looked pretty. My father looked over his glasses when I came into the living room where he was reading, acknowledging that I looked "proper." My mother thought I looked "nice."

The guy, Billy Callahan, picked me up and handed me a nondescript corsage, letting me try to pin it on myself, then acted clumsy and embarrassed when he came in to meet my parents. I thought I smelled beer on his breath. He walked ahead of me on the way to the car, not saying anything, not even that I looked nice. I saw he was with one of his friends and his date when he opened the door to the back seat. We got in and Billy handed me a beer, which I refused, so he kept it and drank it along with the one he already had open. All three of them appeared to have already been drinking. They were talking loud, laughing, and joking, the radio blaring some rock music. I hadn't ever drunk alcohol before. I didn't know what to do or how to act. It was all making me feel nervous and afraid, so I tightened up my seatbelt and sat with my hands in my lap, fiddling nervously with my fingers, eyes downcast. It was horrible. I felt trapped, terribly small and out of place, realizing I had made a huge mistake, wanting to go back home before the night had even begun.

Neither of us said more than a few words to each other on the way. It got worse when we got to the dance. I didn't know how to dance very well and was very self-conscious. Finally, after trying for few minutes, Billy got frustrated, told me I was a pathetic loser and to get away from him, turned his back to me, and walked away, leaving me stunned in the middle of the dance floor. Everyone around us heard him and started to laugh. He went over and talked to his friends who all began staring at me and laughing. I couldn't move. I stood there, stunned, not knowing what to do. I was finally able to walk off the floor through a crowd of dancers, all looking and laughing at me. I hung my head. I thought I might throw up. Tears were starting to well.

I went to the restroom and looked at myself in the mirror, trying to take deep breaths to calm myself, chastising myself for being so stupid to put myself in this position. Calmed down as best as I could, my eyes dried, I went out to find my girlfriends, none of whom had dates, and found them sitting by themselves in a corner. They were sympathetic, but I suspected that they wanted to say "We told you so." We were bored so we all left before it was even nine. Thankfully, my parents were out so I didn't have to explain anything. I went to my room and ripped off my dress and threw it in a pile in the corner, then fell onto my bed, sobbing into a pillow, hating myself for my stupidness and clumsiness. It occurred to me that I was probably a last chance choice for Billy Callahan's prom date.

Thank god there were only two awful weeks after the prom until graduation. Billy Callahan and his friends spread the word of what a dud I was. I became the laughingstock of the school. I didn't even want to go to my graduation, but my parents insisted. I left immediately after the ceremony and skipped the few parties I was invited to. Billy Callahan was the last guy I went out with until I was in law school.

I graduated from high school with honors, completed college in three years, graduating magna cum laude. As in high school, I spent most of my time studying or at the library, and skipping the social life of most undergrads. I was accepted into law school at the University of Iowa, where I met Russell Henderson at a small party in my second year.

CHAPTER 2

Russell was like me in many ways: studious, smart, and very driven—no, extremely driven to succeed. He got his MBA, determined to make a million dollars by the time he reached thirty. I hadn't ever really dated many guys so I guessed that was a good thing, like all guys were like that. But he was nice and treated me with respect. He was the first guy I ever kissed. I think I was the first woman he ever kissed, and it was awkward, very awkward. But I felt safe with him because we were the same.

We got on well together, spending as much time with each other as we could, considering our huge study loads. I went with him a few times to his family's farm. His parents, like mine, seemed conservative. The first time I met them, his mother ran me through the wringer with her questions, frightening me. I didn't like her at all. His brother, Donny, came across as a pompous ass, but his sister, Karen, seemed sweet, though very shy. With Russell being the youngest, it surprised me that both siblings still lived at home. Russell explained that Donny, the oldest, worked on the farm and Karen worked for the local implement dealer. Russell explained that being there were few, if any, places for a single person to rent in the small town, she still camped out with her parents.

I think we both felt that this might be the best we could do, so we decided to get married, which made both sets of parents happy, seeing we were both marrying well educated partners and should get on quite well in our lives.

There wasn't any premarital sex. I wouldn't have known what to do anyway. When I got up the courage to ask my mother, she just scoffed and said it was just the woman's duty to satisfy her husband's needs and dropped the subject. I knew a little about sex from my friends, but had no idea about the mechanics of it all, so I found two books explaining men, women, and sex. I thought the whole thing rather strange, exposing yourself like that, but it was supposed to be pleasurable . . . That remained to be seen. It all sounded disgusting.

I made the law review and would graduate second in my class. Several prestigious law firms— two in Des Moines, one each in Minneapolis and Kansas City, and one in Cedar Rapids—wanted to hire me as a junior partner. But Russell wanted to go to Chicago, even though I was all ready to take the Iowa bar. I would have liked to stay in the state. But he was offered a great position at a financial bank. He scoffed at wanting to stay in Iowa, and didn't want to go to Missouri or Minnesota either. So Chicago, it was. My opportunities were dismissed. I began to study for the Illinois bar.

Our wedding date was set for the end of June so we could get settled in Chicago before it, and have a week-long honeymoon before he started work. I would try to find some sort of position somewhere. Russell's new employer gave him a nice signing package and salary, so we were able to nicely afford the honeymoon trip and a nice apartment in nice, pricey downtown Chicago. Everything was so very *nice*.

While he was on top of the world with his new work, I was not. I was apprehensive about my future, what I might find, where I might end up.

Chapter 3

I had never been to a big city like Chicago. I was shocked and unnerved by the busyness, the tall buildings, all the people. Our apartment was located a few blocks from Russell's bank. It wasn't close to anything, which made no difference since I had no job. The apartment was on the tenth floor, with big windows, but all I could see were other buildings. It was nice. Not very spacious, but plenty big enough for our needs. We bought new furniture for the bedroom, living room, and kitchen plus a desk for Russell in the second bedroom. Both our parents had given us things like lamps, dishes, and some other necessities. Neither of us had any idea about setting up a house but it somehow all came together.

The next step was the wedding. Both Russell and I wanted a small, quiet, simple affair, but between our parents, the guest list was huge. Most of the invitees were people neither of us had ever met. Be that as it may, the invitations were sent. I had my dress, my mother had hers. We had the rings and managed to find a best man and bridesmaid.

The day came. We had the ceremony. There was a huge reception where we received congratulations from people who we didn't know until we were tired of standing. We clumsily had our first dance, cut the cake, and did all the right things to placate our parents. It was over by 12:30 a.m.

That night, Russell and I took turns undressing and putting on our pajamas in the bathroom. We were too uncomfortable and embarrassed to do it in front of each other. Russell was pretty drunk and fell into bed, instantly asleep. I crawled in, maintaining as much distance as I could from him in the king-size bed. I lay awake a long while, thinking about what I had done and wondering what the future might hold. I felt relieved that we had postponed the sex.

We flew out of Des Moines the next day for our honeymoon in Cancun. Russell had insisted we be by the ocean and wanted to go down to a resort there. I told him it was summer and would be really hot. It was in the low nineties and he got sunburned the first day on the beach. He was miserable.

We tried to have sex for the first time on the second night. He just got on top of me, shoved himself into me. It hurt like a hot poker was being rammed into me. He was inside of me for about a minute, grunted, his body stiffening, and then he rolled off, rolled over, and went to sleep. That was far from what those books had told me. It was certainly not pleasurable, but painful and messy. We had sex once more that week and it was awful and painful every time we did it from then on. I hated sex but felt it my duty as a wife.

I spent most of the honeymoon studying for the Illinois bar exam, and Russell spent his reading through a bundle of information from his new employer, most of the time being spent indoors because the sun was so blistering hot. I would have just as soon been back home in our new place in Chicago.

CHAPTER 4

Russell started work the day after we returned home. I spent the day unpacking, finding a grocery store, and stocking up. I hated driving in the Chicago traffic. Plus, I had to take everything up an elevator. I saw another resident with a cart and put it on my list of things to buy.

Russell was home at six, pleased to find dinner almost ready and wine chilling in the fridge. He poured himself a glass and turned on the television, only commenting that his day was all right after I asked him. Other than that, there wasn't much conversation. Nothing about how my day was, where I found the groceries, how nice the place looked. Nothing. I poured myself a large glass of wine and went to the kitchen to finish dinner, remembering that he hadn't talked much when we were dating, and realized I probably shouldn't expect anything different now. It was just like my parents.

The next days and weeks went by with studying for the bar exam which I had signed up to take in late August. Some days I went out exploring the area, looking in the windows of expensive shops on Michigan Avenue, strolling along Lake Michigan, and enjoying almond croissants and dark coffee at a Parisian bakery a block from the apartment.

Russell was already working nine- and ten-hour days, five days a week, and a few hours on Saturdays as well. He was too tired to go out much, and thankfully, to want sex. We managed to go to a few movies and have dinner out every so often. I was able to drag him to the Art Institute one Saturday, and I could tell he was bored silly. We left early but I went back a week later during the week, by myself, and spent all day there viewing the extensive collection of art and wishing deep down that I had studied art instead of law.

I began looking for work, dropping my resume off at various law offices that did family law, especially divorce cases. I was particularly interested in working with women. Of course, I would have to pass the bar first.

August came and I took the exam, awaiting the results with a week of hand-wringing anticipation. I received the registered letter on a Friday morning, set it on the kitchen counter, and stared at it for a long time before I mustered up the courage to open it. I had passed. I was now licensed to practice law in the state of Illinois.

I called Russell at work, which he had told me never to do, but I was so excited I did anyway. He was in a meeting and was not to be disturbed. So I called my parents who acted like "why wouldn't you pass it?" I opened a bottle of wine and waited for Russell to come home. He called at six and said he was going to have dinner with a client and would be home late. I didn't bother to tell him my news. I ordered out for pizza and finished the bottle of wine watching a Netflix movie. Such was my celebration.

CHAPTER 5

After another month of job searching, I had three interviews, one with the District Attorney's Office. I was offered a position, which I accepted. Although it certainly wasn't my first choice, it was a job and I would gain experience. I started work the following Monday.

Russell was happy for me but had to tell me that the DA job wasn't the best I could do and I should have tried harder. My parents felt the same way. At this point, I didn't care. I was employed and was getting really tired of Russell and his distance from me. But he was too tired most of the time to want any sex, which was always a welcome relief. I wondered if this was the way all marriages were. I thought of my parents being more like acquaintances than the couples I saw in the movies or on television. This was probably as good as it would ever be.

I was received with open arms at the DA's office on my first day. There were a number of junior lawyers who acted happy I was joining them. I met again with the District Attorney. The first time had been my interview. He welcomed me and showed me to my cubicle. He introduced me to Glenda, the senior attorney I would be working for, a short, squat woman I guessed to be in her forties. She looked tired and worn-out, but contrary to my first impression, she proved to be a ball of energy and fun to work for. She explained how our working relationship would be, handed me two briefs to research, and directed me to the human resources office where I filled out all the paperwork for my employment. Still wanting a bit of independence, I had opened a separate bank account and had my pay deposited there. I would be happy later that I made that decision. Back at my cubicle, I went to work.

The cases were more interesting than I had anticipated. Glenda was helpful and her guidance was invaluable. I liked her and the other members of our team. I seemed to fit in, was loving my work, and was learning and producing more every day.

Several weeks passed. My coworkers kept inviting me to join them after work on Fridays for drinks and maybe dinner. I felt obligated to Russell and always begged off. But he was hardly ever home until late, most of the time, and had usually already eaten. So the next Friday when I was asked out after work, I accepted. We went to a sports bar that was a regular watering hole for the group. And it was fun. I enjoyed talking and laughing. Most of the group were around my age. Most were single. I had several glasses of wine and was about ready to call a taxi to go home, but everyone insisted I stay and have dinner with them. I walked in the apartment around nine thirty, well fed on a burger and fries and still a bit tipsy. Russell wasn't home, so I went to bed, read for a few minutes, and fell asleep. From then on, Friday nights were my nights to go out and enjoy my life.

About a month later, I got home after my Friday night outing and Russell was already there, steamed that I wasn't home when he arrived. He was really pissed that I hadn't checked with him whether this would be okay. Whether he might approve. I had had a bit too much wine and was feeling pretty silly and laughed, telling him I would go out partying with my colleagues whenever I wanted and that he should grow up. That didn't go very well. He told me I shouldn't be out like that, that I was a married woman and it wasn't right, it could reflect badly on him. My giddiness immediately turned to anger and I told him that I couldn't care less what he thought or about how I might reflect on him, that he was never home, that he was being a pompous ass, that I was just out having fun and enjoying my friends, and he could go to hell. It went downhill from there. I went crying into the bedroom and locked the door, screaming that he could sleep on the couch.

I tried to reconcile the next morning by telling him how I felt about him never being home or us being together, about how he was constantly working or taking clients to dinner—all to which he replied that it was required for his work and that I was being selfish. He was working too hard to waste time having fun and maybe I wasn't working hard enough. My reconciliation turned to anger. I left and went out for a stroll by the lake to cool down. The next few weeks were filled with tension, and I was thankful I hardly saw him. The only time I ever did see him was in the morning when we both were rushing off to our jobs. At night I made it a point to try to be asleep when he got in.

Russell wanted us to go see his parents for a weekend every month or so. They were within an easy three-and-a-half-hour drive. Des Moines was another two hours so I hardly ever saw my family, unless I made it a point to fly there. Russell only went with me the first two times and always seemed to be too busy after that. After two years, I stopped going with him to visit his except for maybe some holidays. I always wondered what they thought, what excuses he told them.

I had no one to talk to about our problems, so I carried all my anger and confusion inside. Things finally settled down after those first few weeks, but things had changed between us. It seemed as if Russell was wary of me now and even more disconnected, as if that were possible. From then on, for the next several years, we were living apart under the same roof. I was miserable and poured myself into my work and my colleagues. Then I met Jessica Morgan, an expert witness for a case I was working on. She changed my life in ways I would never have imagined.

Chapter 6

Jess Morgan was an expert witness for an art theft case I was helping prosecute. She ran a gallery specializing in old lithographic prints. She was single, in her late thirties, tall, elegant, beautiful, and confident.

The case involved the theft of several prints from a private collection by a Chicago industrialist, and we met to discuss the case several times over three weeks, generally after six when she had closed up shop for the day. A few times we met over dinner or drinks and after discussing nuances of the case, we would talk of other things and about ourselves.

She was a native of Chicago. She had studied at the University of Illinois at Urbana-Champaign and earned her PhD in art history at Columbia in New York. Her father, a successful businessman, had died in a small airplane crash in Alaska when she was in college. Her mother still lived in Chicago, but she indicated they weren't very close. She had a brother in New York City and a sister in Portland, Oregon, both married with two children each.

She wanted to know more about me and I gave her the bare basics and moved on. Another night she asked about my marriage, but I dodged her question by changing the subject.

Then, one Friday night, Russell went to his parents for the weekend. He left straight from work, right after lunch. He had insisted I go with him, but I refused and went on to ask him how he could take off work early so easily to go spend time with his parents but never to spend time with me. He responded that he saw me all the time. I said the time he thought he spent with me was worthless, that I wanted his attention, to do things together. It turned into a full-blown fight and he left with me crying.

Feeling alone, sad, and needing some company, I called Jess. She was free, so we made plans to meet for dinner. I ended up having one drink too many and my tongue was pretty loose. When she prodded me again about my marriage, I let go and told her how unhappy I was, and that I regretted ever getting married. Once started I couldn't stop. I told her about our fight that afternoon and every last sordid detail of my lonely life. I was bordering on tears by the time I finished my story. She reached across the table and took my hands, assuring me that that was not the way my life should be, that I should not have to be unhappy and feel alone, that marriage should be a partnership of love, sharing, enjoying time with each other, and having fun. I asked how she knew so much, not ever have been married. She just said that the right person hadn't come along and changed the subject.

Her kindness and the alcohol pushed me then into full-blown sobs. She paid our bill and got me out of the restaurant, insisting I spend the night at her condo rather than going home by myself, in the shape I was in. There was nothing left in me to resist her, so I walked with her guiding and supporting me, my head on her shoulder, the one block back to her place, on the second floor above her gallery.

We went in and I collapsed on her leather sofa and continued my crying jag. She brought over a box of tissues and took me in her arms and held me while I cried every tear I had needed to shed over all the years of my marriage. When my crying subsided into whimpers, she took me to her guest room, showed me the bathroom, gave me a nightgown, and helped me undress and get into bed. I fell instantly asleep, both from the alcohol and from being spent from crying.

I awoke in the morning confused in the strange room, not knowing where I was. The memory of last night started to return, and the more I remembered, the more ashamed and stupid I felt. I checked the bedside clock. It was nine thirty. I had a huge headache. Then the smell of coffee wafted in, along with a rap on the door. I heard Jess ask if I was awake. She came in with a steaming cup and sat on the edge of the bed, touching my face tenderly, asking how I was feeling.

I told her about my head, so she got two aspirin and a glass of water. She was mothering me, and I loved her for it. I needed that more than I had realized. I tried to apologize for last night, but she gave me a warm hug and said it was fine, that she was happy I confided in her and not to worry. She gave me a squeeze and left me to dress and join her for breakfast.

I was surprisingly hungry and was treated to a breakfast of orange juice, bacon, eggs, toast, and more coffee. She suggested we spend the day together and see the new exhibit at the Art Institute. With the aspirin, coffee, and food, I was feeling better. We took a cab back to my apartment so I could change into more casual clothes and comfortable shoes. Then we spent a great day together and we had pizza and watched a movie at her spacious, modern condo with beautiful art and furnishings.

I met her again the next day, and we spent Sunday together walking down by the lake, enjoying the spring weather after another long, cold, dismal Chicago winter. She took my hand several times as we walked. I felt like a young girl again. Later that afternoon she walked me back to my apartment and we made plans to meet for dinner on Wednesday night.

I arrived home mid afternoon, happy with my new friend, who was exciting, smart, fun to be with, and fun to talk to. I liked her a lot. Then Russell came in and my happiness immediately faded. He was pissed. His parents were upset that I wasn't with him again and had accused him of failing in his marriage, of not keeping his wife in line. He told them that he wasn't failing his marriage and would make sure I'd be with him the next visit.

I retorted that I was not going to spend my time being around his meddling, controlling mother, and I would certainly not be with him next time. I went on to again say how unhappy I was with him not ever being around or doing things together, that I was lonely and felt ignored, and that he could take off work to be with his parents and not with me. With that, he glared at me for a long moment, turned with his nose in the air, and went to bed. The way he'd looked at me, I fully expected him to hit me. I took a big breath and slept on the couch. In the morning, I got up and left early for work so as not to have to see him more than in brief passing.

CHAPTER 7

We spent a chilly few weeks in our apartment after that Sunday night. We weren't speaking and avoided each other as best we could. I made him sleep on the couch and I left early in the mornings so as to avoid him as best I could. Of course, he worked late, so I rarely saw him at night.

I met Jess for dinner on Wednesday night, as we had planned. I told her all about the fight. It was good to be able to talk with someone about my marriage and my unhappiness. She and I began to meet for lunch several times a week and had dinner together two or three nights a week. Some nights she would invite me to her condo after work for dinner and maybe a movie. We would sit together on her couch. One night she put her arm around me and pulled me close to her. I happily responded and snuggled in next to her. It made me feel warm and secure, knowing I had such a close friend.

My colleagues were wondering why I wasn't joining them for the office Friday nights. I told them my husband and I had decided on Friday night after-work dates.

In August, Russell left for a corporate retreat in Florida. He would be gone the whole week, from Sunday through the following Sunday. I was elated that he would be out of my hair and that I would be able to spend more time with Jess. I was feeling closer to her than I had ever felt with my husband.

He left early Saturday for a late-morning flight, so I had made a date with Jess for the afternoon and evening. We had drinks, followed by dinner, followed by a nightcap at her place. She closed the door behind us, took my hand and pulled me to her and held me. She whispered in my ear that she was falling in love with me. I shuddered, confused about what she meant. I knew I cared for her as a friend, but what did she mean? I pulled away and she saw the stunned look in my eyes.

"I'm sorry," she said. "That was wrong of me to say, to say it that way without any explanation. I thought you must have figured it out, that I'm a lesbian and I'm attracted to women. I'm really attracted to you. Really, really attracted."

"I know what a lesbian is. I thought you wanted to be my friend, not lover," I said more harshly than I had intended, but deep down I felt a warmth rise into my heart that I hadn't ever felt before. Not with Russell, not with anyone. So many feelings then arose. Jess was the only person who'd ever said they loved me. I began to feel dizzy. I liked being with her. Maybe I could be in love with her too, but didn't realize it.

"I'm sorry," I stammered. "I . . . I'm just a little overwhelmed right now. I'm not sure what I'm feeling. I'm very flattered to know you care for me. I care for you too. You're very special to me, but I don't know about loving another woman. I'm just not sure what I feel right now." Then I hugged her back. I hugged her tight, and my eyes began to tear up, and I struggled not to cry.

She pulled back, then leaned in and kissed me. I kissed her back. Then she pulled away again, pushed me to arm's length, and said, "I'm sorry, I shouldn't have done that. It was wrong of me. You are vulnerable. I'm sorry."

I looked at her for a moment, then said, "It's okay. Really. I liked it. It meant a lot to me." And I drew her to me and kissed her back, feeling a warm sensation of never-before-felt desire rising up inside me.

She led me to her bedroom, where we slowly undressed each other, kissing and caressing and falling into her bed. I felt sensations that were totally new. I was twenty-nine years old and had my first orgasm that night.

CHAPTER 8

I spent every night that week at Jess's condo, only going to the apartment for clothes and necessities. I was giddy with the excitement of being with someone who I felt honestly cared for me. Sharing a life with another woman? It was a very strange concept for me to wrap my brain around. It didn't seem right. It was against everything I'd ever been taught to believe. I felt it odd to even think about being with a woman. I had never thought of myself as being gay. Maybe I wasn't gay. Maybe I was bisexual or something else. Or just needed to have relief from a dead marriage.

How was I attracted to her? Sexually? Yes! Emotionally? Yes! As a friend? Yes, yes, yes to everything! My brain was in turmoil at the thought of all this. But in truth, I hadn't ever been this attracted to anyone, male or female. I was always too busy to ever allow myself that luxury.

When I told Jess of my feelings, she said that all she wanted was for me to be happy and that she hoped she could be part of my life. She then went on to tell me that she'd had several relationships over the years and was fully aware of the difficulties in any relationship, but simply wanted for me to be happy no matter what I decided about my sexuality . . . or her. Plus, I was still married, sadly . . . Still married to a man I had no feelings for.

Yes, there was Russell. He had texted me that he and several others were going to corporate headquarters in New York after the retreat in Atlanta for some new training. I was overjoyed that I would have another week of freedom to be with Jess. The thought of him coming home made me feel sick to my stomach.

I told Jess and asked her if I could keep hanging out with her at her place.

"Of course! You're welcome. I'm thrilled we can have another week. But then what?"

"Thanks. But then what? Yeah, then what? I don't know. Everything is so messed up. Every time I think of having to go back to that apartment, I feel sick to my stomach. Sometimes I just feel so tired, I don't know if I can go on."

Jess asked, "Then why don't you leave him? Get a divorce, get free of this guy who you can't stand to be around. Get free of him and get on with your life."

"I don't know if I could, or how I could. It would be a major disaster and I don't know if I can deal with all the drama. He's so programmed to never fail at anything, he'd see this as a monumental disaster in his life. I'm not sure what would happen and, if you get right down to it, I'm afraid he might react violently. I wouldn't want to be around him when he found out."

"One of my clients is a divorce attorney. She owes me a big favor for a rare print I found her for a song. Would you mind if I contact her to see if she'll meet with you?"

I hesitated for a moment. My heart was pounding with this possibility I could never have before considered. But now? Maybe I could leave him, be free from this marriage. I had often wanted to leave Russell, but never thought it could be a reality. I had no idea how I'd ever do it, how to do it, what I'd do. And now, with Jess's support, maybe it could happen. I thought about it for a moment.

"Yeah, I'd like that. Call her and see. I'd be happy to meet with her if she has time."

"Good. I'll call her tomorrow," she said.

I got an appointment for one o'clock on Thursday of that week. I took that afternoon off from work and went to meet Cynthia Carpenter, Attorney at Law, specializing in divorce.

I was greeted by a receptionist in her tenth-floor downtown office about seven blocks from the DA's office. I waited in the elegantly appointed reception area and was offered coffee, tea, or water. I asked for tea.

A few moments later, before I had any chance to check messages and emails on my phone, Cynthia came out of her office, introduced herself, escorted me into her office, and offered me a seat in a plush leather chair. She took a seat across a small coffee table, sat back, and crossed her legs, making a tent with her fingers and looking at me warmly.

I guessed her to be in her mid to late fifties. She was not tall but had a presence that filled the room and I immediately sensed she was not someone to mess with. She had bobbed dark hair and was neither attractive nor unattractive. She just was. I immediately liked her. I caught myself wondering if she was a lesbian, but then I saw a huge diamond on the ring finger of her left hand.

The receptionist brought in a pot of tea, two cups with saucers, and a selection of sweeteners, from stevia to white sugar. We chatted a bit about ourselves to get more comfortable and familiar, then we got down to business.

"So, tell me about your marriage," she said.

I went on to tell her everything from day one to present time, leaving nothing out. Cynthia stopped me every so often to ask a question to clarify some area. She was writing notes as we went and had also asked permission to record the conversation.

Maybe an hour later, I had finished my saga and the tea.

"Want to take a minute to stretch? Do you need the restroom? More tea?" she asked.

I did have to use the restroom and it felt good to move. I realized I'd made it through the whole time without crying. I returned and sat down to a fresh pot of tea, a small assortment of cookies, and a glass of water with ice and lemon. It hit me that we had not yet discussed fees and with this sort of treatment, I doubted she would be inexpensive. My question was answered when she rejoined me.

"Okay," she began. "I'll be happy to take your case. You certainly need to be done with this marriage and have a life. Now, my normal fee is five hundred dollars per hour, and I normally spend anywhere from ten to twenty or more hours, depending on how difficult the other party decides to be. However, I owe a big favor to your friend, Jess, and she is calling it in, so I'll take you on pro bono."

I was stunned and responded vehemently, "I can't let you do that! Maybe lower your hourly for me or something, but I want to be fair with you."

"I appreciate your offer, but I'm happy to do it, as I said, pro bono."

We haggled for a few more minutes, finally

settling on a flat twenty-five hundred for everything.

I explained again how afraid I was of Russell. Cynthia told me to set up a time to move out, taking what was mine. She'd have the divorce papers served the next day. In the meantime, she'd draw up a restraining order and have it ready if there were any problems. Also, he would be told in the filing that he would not have any direct contact with me. Any contact would be through his attorney and only through his attorney, if he decided to retain one. It would take her about two weeks to get all the paperwork ready to be filed.

"So what do you want for a settlement? From what you have told me, Russell has earned a good sum, and his future earning potential looks to be very good. How much do you think he is currently worth?"

I thought for bit and replied, "He likes to brag about it. The last time he did was a few months ago. He mentioned the sum of over six or seven million."

"Wow. You could be entitled to a lot of money. Any major debts?"

"No. None I am aware of. He's very frugal."

"Hmm, no children? You're an associate in the DA's office? I'm aware of what associates' salaries are over there, so I know he pulls in way more than you do. Did either of you bring more than the other into the marriage?"

"Russell got a nice signing bonus with Americo. I was unemployed for close to six months, but before I graduated, I had good offers from law firms in other cities than Chicago. I turned them down to move here with him."

"Okay, so you gave up a more lucrative career somewhere else to move here?"

"Yes, that's correct. I had some really great offers from some good law firms to enter as a junior partner in family law, which is what I wanted to practice. I made the law review when I graduated law school and was in demand."

"Okay then, in that case, I can see probably going for several mill, even though he had the signing bonus to begin with. Maybe two point five or three million? What do you think?"

"I think he'd fight that much. I don't want a fight or to have to go to court. I really want to avoid a court battle. Maybe half a million?"

"I understand your concern, but don't sell yourself short. So how about two million? Somehow, I doubt he will contest that. It's more than equitable, and any attorney would advise him to settle instead of going to court. Any judge would most likely give you a larger amount, maybe even alimony, given his wealth and your lower salary. You'd be foolish to ask for any less."

I considered this while having a cookie and some more tea. "You think we can do this then, without any hassle? I couldn't handle his drama, having to see him in court. Once I move out, I just want it done and to never have to see him ever again."

"Of course, there are no guarantees, but chances are he'll sign off without having to go to court. He'd be stupid to not to. And any decent attorney would advise him so."

"Then let's do it, and the sooner the better. I can certainly live with two million."

Cynthia asked me to specifically itemize anything I wanted to take with me. All I wanted were some things my parents had given us that were important to me, along with my clothes and personal items. I wanted nothing to do with any of the rest of it. I just wanted to be free. I signed some papers and it was put in motion. I only had to decide when to have him served.

CHAPTER 9

It was after Thanksgiving, which Russell thankfully ignored because he was too busy, so I got to spend the day with Jess. The divorce papers were ready to go. It was a matter of my deciding when. I was petrified. Russell was his usual self—distant, even more so since we'd been having the fights about seeing parents and some other disagreements more and more frequently. He was angry and didn't speak to me for a week after I refused to go with him the last time he went to see his parents. He suspected something was going on. I couldn't believe it, but I was having an extramarital affair. I had seen movies and TV shows about such things, and here I was, acting out my own indiscretions.

I hadn't been to see my parents in a long time and decided I needed to go to tell them in person about my impending divorce, rather than by a phone call or email. Jess said she'd go with me. We flew out on a Friday afternoon after a fierce fight with Russell about me going. It was nothing new. It seemed we fought over everything these days.

Once in the air, I took a deep breath and ordered a glass of wine. My mother would pick us up at the airport. She was already wondering why I was bringing a friend instead of my husband. As they say, the shit was going to hit the fan, and I wasn't looking forward to it. Thank god Jess was with me for moral support.

We got into Des Moines at nine fifteen, so we grabbed some fast food on the way back to the house, and after saying hi to my dad, we crawled into bed. I was stressed out and wanted to talk to Jess, but she was in the other guest room. I thought better of it so my folks might not suspect what was going on with us. Eventually I drifted off to sleep.

Saturday, we spent making small talk. I took Jess out for a tour of Des Moines and the newer shopping area by the capitol. Later Saturday afternoon we had had cocktails with Mom and Dad, both their usual aloof selves. Jess was her charming self. I was nervous as a cat on a hot tin roof. Mom excused herself to prepare some dinner and I joined her in the kitchen. I began making a salad while Mom was getting some steaks ready for Dad to grill and potatoes to bake in the oven.

"Mom, I need to tell you something. Something that isn't easy for me."

"Oh my god! You're pregnant?"

I laughed nervously. "No, that's not it at all. I'm divorcing Russell, Mom. I'm getting a divorce. My marriage is awful and I'm getting a divorce. There, it's out."

She paused what she was doing and didn't say a word for what seemed like hours, grasping for words. Then she blurted out, "This is such a shock! I don't know what to say! What are you thinking? What do his parents say? Have you tried counseling? Your father . . . I can't imagine what he'll say. What our friends will say. Our pastor. We'll be looked at as failures. This just can't be happening. Isn't there something to do, work things out somehow? Why?"

"Mom, I'm sorry, but this isn't about you or what your friends will think. I've made up my mind. I'm going to leave him and that's that. Marrying him was a huge mistake from the get-go."

"But, Dana, what do your friends think?"

"Mom, that's one of the problems with being with Russell. I have no friends. We have no friends. He has no friends that I'm aware of, anyway."

"Oh, Dana! This is so disappointing. You seemed so happy. And this Jess person? What about her? Who's she to you? I see the way looks at you, and I think she's more than just a friend."

I took a breath and said, with maybe too much defensiveness, "She's just a friend, Mom! She knows what is going on and she's the only one who I can talk to and depend on. She, at least, gives me gives me some support."

"You don't have to be so defensive! I thought you and Russell were happy together."

"I was never happy with him. I just existed. Simply existed from day to day. He doesn't support my career or any of my wants or needs. We fight over me not wanting to go to see his parents. He was angry I came here. He gets angry over everything these days. It's awful being around him. We never talk. We never do anything. We never did anything. We haven't slept together for almost a year. I'm tired of it."

I started to cry. My mother huffed, said no more, and continued to prepare for dinner. Dinner was filled with tension and didn't relax until we left on Sunday, when we escaped and took a taxi to the airport. I never told my father, leaving it to my mother to figure it out. I was pissed at her. Jess was a great sounding board while I consumed too many glasses of wine on our short flight home. I was fairly wasted when I was dropped off at our apartment.

Jess parked and turned to me. "I'd like it if you would move in with me after the divorce. I'd really like it if you would."

I was not prepared for this. I took a moment and stammered, "I need time . . . time to sort through this."

"But where will you go? Stay with me, then, until you can find another place, if you decide, when the time comes. I don't want to pressure you."

"Okay. I'll come to your place when I move out. Then we'll see. Thanks, Jess. I appreciate all your help and understanding."

With that, I gave her a peck on the cheek and reluctantly went to the apartment. Thankfully Russell was out, so I showered and went to bed.

Before I went to sleep, a wave of anger came over me, and I decided to give Russell a present for his birthday on December 13th: the divorce papers. "Happy birthday, Russell."

CHAPTER 10

Two years later

I did go to Jess's when I left Russell. I never left. I felt happier than I had ever been. Jess was a great companion, although her business required her to be gone a lot, mainly to Europe where the antique prints were. She was in Paris most of the time, either for a sale or to examine some prints close up to determine authenticity and provenance. I was on my own much of the time.

I had found a new position in a family practice law firm, where I was able to do what I'd always wanted. My new colleagues were great. We normally went out for drinks and sometimes dinner after work on Fridays, whenever Jess wasn't home. Thankfully, I never again heard from Russell. My parents weren't speaking to me. But I felt freer, happier, and more alive than ever.

One Sunday morning, I was going through the *Chicago Times*'s Sunday supplement, scanning for upcoming events, when I spotted an ad for a folk music club Jess and I went to, on occasion, for some acoustic music and obscure but talented singer-songwriters. A San Francisco-based folk trio called the Stealth Movers would be appearing for a three-night run in two weeks. The name caught my eye, and I read the description of the group made up of singer-songwriter Hannah Morse, Russell Henderson, guitar, mandolin, and vocals, and Miguel (Mick) Espinoza on bass and vocals.

I reread it several times, wondering. *No, no way. It can't be him.* I had heard through my attorney that he had left the city and moved back to Iowa, but I had heard nothing more for almost two years. Jess was down at the gallery catching up on a few things. I went to my laptop and did a search for the Stealth Movers. I found their website along with several reviews and some YouTube videos. I watched two of the videos and, yup. There he was, playing music with a very talented female singer and a tall Mexican man on bass. This Russell had long hair and tanned features, dressed in blue jeans and an untucked, loose-fitting buttoned shirt, open at the neck with rolled-up sleeves, and with some sort of choker necklace. He looked healthier than I could ever remembered him being. And he was good on both guitar and mandolin. *My god, this is the anal-retentive jerk I married and divorced? Unbelievable.* I was watching the videos again when Jess came in.

"Hey, who's that? They sound really good."

I stammered, "You won't fucking believe this. Fucking unbelievable. Just fucking unbelievable. Take a look."

"My god. It's him? What the hell? They're really good. We have got to go see them. I'll get tickets for the first night. Maybe all three nights. This is crazy weird, from all you ever told me about him. What happened to the geeky guy you divorced?"

I was speechless, feeling like I was in some sort of time warp. This man who was a complete Type-A jerk was playing in a folk trio. Finally, I said, "I have no idea. Absolutely no idea. He looks so different. He actually looks like he's having fun. And look at his hair. This is all very strange."

We got tickets for all three nights. I didn't care. If we needed to, we could always give them away. But I needed to experience all that I could of whatever had happened to this guy.

The night of the first show seemed never to come. I was beside myself trying to understand what had happened to him. Jess and I crowded into the dark club. The seating consisted of small tables that sat four. It was a small, intimate venue that seated fewer than a hundred people. Wine, beer, coffee, and munchies were all available. Jess and I each ordered a glass of wine and sat back and waited. Another couple joined us right at seven thirty, when a voice came over the sound system announcing the Stealth Movers. The three of them walked onto the stage. And there he was, Russell Henderson in the flesh, long hair, untucked shirt, khaki shorts, running shoes, tanned arms and legs and all.

They jumped into their first song. I immediately fell in love with the woman singer. Her voice was beautiful. The instrumentation was perfect and Russell was, I don't know . . . interesting? I looked over the crowd and I spotted his sister, Karen. What was she doing here? Maybe she came in from Iowa to see them. But she looked busy as she shuffled around and then disappeared behind the stage.

The first set flew by and I was already happy we had gotten tickets for the next nights. These folks were good. Most of their music was original, with a few covers thrown in. The original tunes, I guessed, were written by the woman, Hannah. Her lyrics of love, loss, times, and places struck a chord in me and I found myself choking up with emotion several times. We ordered more wine and waited for the next set.

Another long set and two encore songs, and after they announced that their three CDs and T-shirts would be for sale in the lobby, they were done. We ordered more wine and waited for crowd to thin out. After things settled, we went toward the lobby, and there was Karen, sitting behind the merch table, selling T-shirts and CDs as fast as she could.

"Hello, Karen," I said as I stood in front of her. She was busy sorting cash and when she looked up, her mouth dropped open and her eyes about popped out.

She was finally able to stammer, "Oh my god, Dana. You came! You actually came to see these guys, to see Russell? Oh my god . . . Never expected you to show up. Holy crap. Wait 'til Russell knows. Oh my god."

I smiled at her. "How are you, Karen? It's great to see you. This is Jess."

She looked over, smiled, and offered her hand. Jess took it and smiled back. "Nice to meet you, Karen."

I sort of blurted out, "What are you doing here with them? You're married and have those two little boys, bigger now after a few years?"

"Oh, Dana. So much has happened, so much. My husband left me right after you and Russell, well, after your divorce. I'm with Mick, the bass player, and am sort of their manager. I've never had so much fun in all my life as traveling around with those three crazies."

"Crazies? With all due respect, Russell was one of

the most uptight people I ever knew. Crazy wasn't in his vocabulary."

"I'll let him explain. Here they come now."

And there they were: Hannah, Russell, and Mick. I thought Russell's jaw was going to hit the floor and his eyes were going to pop out of their sockets.

"Holy shit, Dana. What are you doing here?"

"We came to hear some good music. You three are amazing. We have tickets for all three nights and plan on being here. Hi, Hannah. I love your voice and your music. All of you were great."

She looked at me for a moment, and smiled with a twinkle. "So you're Dana? Nice to meet you," she said, offering her hand.

And then Mick said, "So you're the ex. Amazing. Thanks for coming. Good to see you."

And I said, "And this is Jess, my partner." Right then, there was enough awkward to go around for the next few years. All six of us stood there for what seemed like an eternity, until Russell finally broke the silence.

"Dana, we're in town for the next few days. Would you consider having lunch or something so we can talk more? I want to catch up with you and your life. It's truly great to see you. You look great. And, Jess, it's nice to meet you. Let's all get together and spend some time. Wow, it is really good to see you, Dana. How about tomorrow? It's Saturday and hopefully you're not working." It was all said with sincerity and a huge smile.

It was my turn for my jaw to drop. This was not the same sullen, self-absorbed, uncaring man I'd been married to. I glanced at Hannah, who was smiling and nodding expectantly. I looked at Jess, who gave me a "sure, go ahead." I nodded and said, "How about eleven thirty at Julio's? It's fun and it'll be slow at noon on a Saturday. Will that work for you?"

"Sounds great. I'll meet you then. Right now, all I want is to hit the sack." He looked at Hannah and gave her a kiss on the cheek. She gave a coy smile and rolled her eyes.

We said our goodnights and parted. In the cab on our way home, Jess asked, "Are you okay? That was extremely strange, from what you told me about him. Are you sure that's the same guy?"

"Hard to believe, but it was certainly Russell Henderson." It was him but not the same guy I was married to. Not the same at all.

Jess left me on my own for lunch. I got to Julio's about eleven forty-five, and there was Russell, waiting in a booth. He waved me over.

Wondering what I was doing meeting him and feeling very nervous, I slid into the booth.

He greeted me with a big, warm smile and said,

"Hi, Dana. You look great. Thanks for coming."

I blurted out, "You . . . you look so different. You seem different. Your hair. Playing music? Really? And . . . San Francisco? So, what's going on? What do your parents think about you?"

"Whoa, one at a time," he said, laughing. "Obviously things have changed a bit."

"A bit? A *bit*? God, what happened, Russell? What happened to the uptight banker I was married to?"

"Well, when you left me—and by the way, I don't blame you—it took me a while, but I realized what an ass I was. I'm sorry for how I treated you. I would have left me. Truth is, I didn't know any better. That's a feeble excuse, I know, but I am truly sorry." He paused for a long moment, looking past me into some other space. "Forgive me?"

"Of course I forgive you. We were both too young and inexperienced in life. We never should have gotten married. I have to say, leaving you was the hardest decision I ever had to make, but I'm happy for both of us that I did. You seem really happy. And Hannah, she seems amazing. I'm guessing you're together?"

The waiter, dressed in the obligatory white shirt, black tie, black vest, pants, and shoes, appeared with water and menus. We each ordered iced tea.

"Yeah, Hannah. She's amazing. We've been

hanging out together a little over two years now. I met her my second day on the road after I, for some unknown reason, decided to go on a camping trip in the west. She was hitchhiking and, believe it or not, I picked her up. To this day, I am surprised that I ever did that. You know as well as anyone what a social derelict I was. She . . ." He paused, and I noticed his lips quiver and his eyes tearing up. Regaining his composure, he continued with a thick voice, "She more or less saved me from myself. I don't think I tell her enough. Anyway, she was the complete opposite of me, a total free spirit, which I discovered early on when we went swimming that first afternoon in Nebraska and she got in the water in her birthday suit."

"What? Oh my god! What did you do?" I said, laughing.

"Turned red as a beet, I'm sure. Looked the other way. Embarrassed to death . . . Didn't phase her, though. But she, I don't really know, but she took me on an amazing adventure, from a sweat lodge, to hiking and exploring, to Buddhism, to music, of course, and to a life I never could have imagined. She taught me about love, not by sitting down and teaching me, but by example. She is an amazing woman who I am very grateful for and very much in love with."

The waiter appeared with our teas and was ready

to take our order. We both cleared our minds and ordered without ever having glanced at the menu. Both of us ordered salads, mine with chicken, Russell's with brisket.

As soon as the waiter left, I asked more excitedly than I wanted, "Are you married?"

"No! That's the farthest thing from our minds. Maybe someday. Her mom and stepfather have been together over twenty years and never married. They're an interesting couple, really. Really interesting. So, enough about me. How are you? How are you, really?"

"I'm good. Really good. Jess, like Hannah, saved me, I guess. She gave me the strength and support during that last year we were together. Without her, I don't know what I'd ever have done. She's good to me. Encourages me, gives me space, supports me. My parents hate her. My father hasn't spoken to me since he found out I divorced you and am with a woman. My mother barely speaks to me. It makes me very sad. But they're locked into their belief system, worried about what their friends and pastor will think, and don't want anything to cause any chinks in their stone walls . . . Sort of like we were, back then. Funny how life works."

"It is truly strange indeed. Back then, if someone had told me I'd be playing music professionally, I'd have laughed in their face. But I love it, and I'm having more fun than I could ever imagine. We even make some money. Are you still at the DA's office?"

"No. Actually, I started with a private firm about six months ago. Family practice, which is what I always wanted. Overall, things are good."

Our food arrived and we ate with smatterings of small talk. As we were finishing, I asked Russell to tell me what had really happened. He hesitated for a moment and went on to tell me how his world fell apart after I left him. He told me about his depression, his mother's unrelenting criticism, and his crazy idea of a solo camping trip. About his loneliness. About Hannah and how they fell in love. About her parents. About Sausalito. About music. About his time at a Buddhist retreat center, and how he had started therapy. About his father's heart attack. About how Donny was really his half brother and was serving time in jail for spousal abuse. About his mother's confession and apologies, and finally about how he would never go back to banking.

I sat there and realized my mouth was hanging open as I tried to absorb this epistle. He was so different now, so open. Our table had been cleaned and when I looked at my watch, we had been talking way over an hour after we had finished eating. We both came out of our trance at the same time and reached for the check at the same time, but Russell insisted it was his treat. The bill was paid and we got up to leave. He took my hand as we walked out into the Chicago sunlight. He turned and looked at me for a minute and I thought, even hoped, he might kiss me. But it was not to be. He said his goodbye with a short hug, turned, and walked away without another word.

I stood watching him as he walked down the street until he disappeared around a corner. My mind was racing with questions. What would have happened if he'd had this epiphany while we were married? Before we were married? Would we still be married? I was now unsure of my decision to leave him. Maybe I should have hung in there. Did I still love him? Did I ever? Doubts about my relationship with Jess unexpectedly erupted. Why was I with her? Did I really love her? Was she just a temporary fix that I kept clinging to? Should I have stayed with Russell? Would he have ever become the man he now was if we were still married? I doubted I'd never know. I kept looking down the empty street and turned to go home. Tears of uncertainty and fear fell onto the city sidewalk I somehow felt a stranger to, a life I now felt a stranger to.

CHAPTER 11

I walked into the condo late in the afternoon after my lunch with Russell. Jess called from the bedroom, where she was busy packing for another European trip to visit auction houses and galleries to look for prints for her gallery. She was originally scheduled to leave the next week, but a rare print she had been looking for had emerged in a gallery in Rome, and the owner, a longtime friend, was holding it for her. She was off to get it before he changed his mind, so she was leaving a week early on a late flight tomorrow.

"How was lunch?" she asked as I walked into the bedroom.

"Okay, I guess. Actually, it was very strange. He's changed so much and I felt . . . Yeah, I felt dumb and uninteresting. He's experienced so much. Done interesting things, let go of his old life. Am I in a rut? Do you think I'm in a rut?"

"No, not at all. You're a successful attorney in a good firm, doing what you have always wanted to do. Why would you think you're in a rut?"

"I don't know. You're right. I am doing what I wanted, I guess. His life isn't my life. He just got me thinking. Maybe we need more adventure. Do some traveling."

"Dana, I have enough adventure and traveling. I'm leaving for seven weeks in Europe for work and I don't think I could handle any more travel or adventure in my life. Maybe you need to take a trip somewhere. Somewhere fun, like the Bahamas? Or maybe someplace in Mexico, like Cozumel?"

"Maybe. Neither sound much fun alone. Never mind. Sorry I brought it up."

"I'm finished packing. Let's go for dinner before the concert tonight. You still want to go, don't you? After your lunch with him, I mean."

"Sure. I really want to hear them again. How about the Mexicali around five thirty? I'll call for reservations. I'm going to lie down and rest for a while," I responded unenthusiastically.

Dana went down to the gallery and I lay down on the bed and closed my eyes. Thoughts kept flooding my head. *Am I happy? Am I really committed to Jess? Am I really a lesbian or does Jess just make me comfortable? Do I need a change in my life? She's leaving for seven weeks. I have no real friends, just a few people from work. I do the same thing again and again, while she runs around Europe . . . Which is absolutely nothing?*

Russell and Hannah, Karen and Mick. They all seem so free and happy. Am I happy? God, Russell is so damn sexy. Was I stupid to let him go? Would he have changed? Probably not . . . Not with me, anyway. I'm not like Hannah. I'm just boring . . .

I must have dozed off. I heard Jess calling me. "Hey, Dana! Time to get ready to go."

I know I was distant during our dinner and the concert. They did all different material from last night and again, it was great. Afterward, we left without waiting around to see them. We didn't talk on the way home and just went to bed. I couldn't sleep. Too many questions were running through my mind. I finally took a sleeping pill at twelve thirty and awoke at eight thirty with Jess gently shaking my shoulder.

"Hey, lazy girl. You going to sleep all day?" she said with forced cheeriness as she handed me a cup of coffee.

I blinked my eyes awake and saw the time. "It's Sunday, a day to sleep in," I said groggily with a sleeping pill hangover.

"Are you okay?" she asked.

"Yeah," I lied. "I just had a hard time getting to sleep so I took a sleeping pill. Coffee'll wake me up."

"You took a whole one? A half is usually enough for you."

"Yeah, a whole one. I know, I know." I wanted to add "Mother" but held my tongue. "What time do you have to leave for the airport?"

"I have a cab coming at three. That'll give me plenty of time for check in, security, and a glass of wine or two before boarding."

She was taking an all-night flight and would sleep. She'd arrive in Rome sometime tomorrow. I usually worried about her flying and when she'd arrive, where she would be staying, if she'd be okay, but this time, none of it seemed to matter. I was ready for her to be gone. I wanted to be by myself. For the first time in three years, I didn't want her around. I wanted to be alone.

I spent the day reading. There was little communication between us . . . an uncomfortable silence. As usual, Jess was going over and over her itinerary, trying to make sure all her time would be well spent and productive. She would have a number of auctions to be prepared for, meetings with gallery owners, drinks, dinners, a whirlwind schedule. Me? I would be here, wondering who the hell I really was.

At three, she took her suitcase and carry-on, gave me a kiss on the cheek, then looked straight into my eyes and asked hesitantly, "Will you be here when I return?"

I couldn't meet her gaze and looked away,

hesitated, and replied, "I don't know, Jess. I'm sorry, but I really don't know."

She took a deep quivering breath, turned, and left.

CHAPTER 12

That night, I went again to see Russell, Hannah, Mick, and Karen. The last night, there was less of a crowd and a number of empty seats. Karen noticed I was by myself and came and sat down with me.

"Where's Jess?" she asked.

I told her about her European business trip.

"So, are you okay with her gone for so long?"

"Yeah, I'm used to it. She usually goes several times a year, most times not as long as this trip. She has a lot lined up for the next few weeks."

"So, do you ever go off on a trip by yourself when she's gone?"

"No, I just get a lot of work done."

"Must be hard knowing she's traipsing around Europe. Does she ever want you to go with her?"

"No. She says I'd be bored and a distraction."

"Oh. Hey, I have to get out to the merch table and get it organized. Enjoy. See you later."

I sat there with my wine, feeling lonely, sad, worried, and wondering. They came onstage and had another great concert, again, with all different material. I admired their professionalism and enthusiasm. They ended with two encores. I walked out and stopped to say goodbye to Karen.

"Hey, we're all going out as soon as everyone's gone. Why don't you come with us?" she asked eagerly.

"No. Thanks for asking, but I don't want to intrude."

"You won't be intruding. Hannah and Mick keep asking about you. They'd love to get to know you. Trust me. You will be more than welcome. Russell kept talking about how great it was to have lunch with you. Come on."

And then the three of them appeared. Mick asked, "Where's Jess? We wanted you two to join us to celebrate a great gig here. Sold out two nights and pretty much sold out of our CDs and T-shirts. Celebration is in order!"

I briefly explained about Jess, and that just made them more enthusiastic about me joining them. "Can't have you going home alone without some partying," Mick said and everyone laughed.

Their insistent enthusiasm was contagious and I reluctantly relented. I helped schlep gear to their large Mercedes cargo van parked behind the venue and we headed to a sports bar Russell knew from his time in Chicago. The van had a comfortable bench seat that sat Hannah, Karen, and myself, while the two guys rode in the front, Russell driving, Mick shotgun. All their gear was stored neatly in shelves on the sides in the cargo area and there was a blow-up mattress for when they needed to do an all-night run. Their energy was infectious. I was laughing with them. For the first time in the last few days, I wasn't thinking about my life. I was having a good time.

We arrived at the bar, and Russell stopped to let us out before he and Mick went to find a parking spot. Since it was Sunday night, the bar was about half-full. I was already planning on calling in sick tomorrow, as I guessed it might be a late night.

We found a large table. The two guys joined us shortly and we ordered a round of drinks and an array of appetizers. They seemed to be so close and happy together and I liked them all. I was envious.

The night wore on with them sharing stories of their time on the road and their homes in California. Hannah and Russell had recently moved into their own place, a two-bedroom cottage a little way inland from the coast, and about a half mile from Hannah's parents. Karen and Mick lived in a one-bedroom north of Sausalito. Their lives sounded full of friends, fun, and a lot of hard work with their music. I became even more envious with my imagination beginning to run wild, making me wonder even more about my own life.

The margaritas, jealousy, and the excitement all combined to make my mind start to flicker like an old black-and-white movie I saw years go. Then I was suddenly overcome by a wave of emotion, both sadness and happiness at once. I felt tears coming and I excused myself and went to the front of the bar and pulled out some tissues.

A moment later, Hannah joined me. "What's wrong, Dana? Did we say something to upset you?"

"Nothing anyone said. It's everything. You all seem so happy and fun. My life is boring. It's going nowhere. I'm sorry. Apparently I'm having a little crisis."

Over the last few days, I was realizing I really didn't like Chicago that much anymore, if I ever truly did. Seeing Russell again and meeting his friends made me look at myself, and I was now feeling unhappy about everything concerning my life. I never wanted to go back to Jess's place again, even though she was somewhere over the Atlantic probably drinking wine and chatting it up with anyone close-by. It wasn't my home. It never was. She never liked any ideas I had, or anything of mine that I wanted to add to the collection of items on shelves or on the walls. There was nothing of me there.

Hannah put her arm around my shoulders and pulled me to her. Her warmth just made me feel worse and I snuggled in and cried on her shoulder.

Karen joined us. "What's going on? Dana? What's wrong?"

I had calmed down enough to tell them what I was feeling.

Karen was the first to respond. "Jess is gone for what, seven weeks? Why don't you take some time off and come with us for a few weeks. You can catch a flight back here whenever you want."

"I couldn't do that. With Russell and everything, he wouldn't want me hanging around. With our history, it would be weird. Awkward. I'd just be in the way."

"No you wouldn't. Russell will be fine with it. I know he will. And so will Mick. Us girls run the show, don't we, Hannah?" Karen said with a smug smile.

"Yup, we make those fellas toe the line. Come on, Dana. This sounds so fun."

Karen said excitedly, "We're leaving tomorrow for a few days at my folks' place and we'll do a gig in Iowa City. Then to Des Moines, Omaha, Lincoln, Denver, Albuquerque, Santa Fe, Durango, Salt Lake, Lake Tahoe and home . . . About three weeks. You can help me at the merch table. It'll be so fun. Come on! Say yes. Please?"

"Wait, hold on. This is too much. I can't go off on the spur of the moment. I need to give more notice.

227

What am I saying? No. This is crazy."

"Tell them it's a family emergency. It's kind of an emergency. And it's sort of like family. You used to be, anyway. Just a little lie. Your firm will never know."

"But it they ever found out . . . I'm a junior partner. I'd be blackballed from ever making partner."

"From what you were saying earlier, do you even want to be partner?" asked Hannah.

Before I could think about an answer, Russell and Mick appeared and Mick asked, "So what's going on here? What are you three conspiring about?"

Karen told them everything we had been talking about.

Mick said, "That'd be cool, having you along. What do you think, Russell?"

"Yeah, that'd be great," he said with a furrow in his brow, but smiling.

"No, it won't work. Thanks for your concern, but no. I'd just be in the way. And going to your parents' house? No thanks. They probably hate me."

Karen said, "They've changed about a hundred and eighty degrees from when you were around. They'd probably love to see you again."

Hannah said, "Oh come on. You won't be in the way. They like having Mick and me around. That says a lot. We have a ton of room in the van. It'd be so nice to have you. Really. How much are you going to make us beg?"

All four of them started talking at once about how fun it would be to have me along, someone new to break the monotony of just the four of them. I shut them all out. I was not going to go with them. I firmly rejected their pleas and called a cab. Before I left, Hannah, Karen and I exchanged contact information. My cab arrived and I left.

I walked into Jess's condo with a new understanding that it was indeed hers and I simply lived there with her to keep her company and give her some pleasure in bed, the latter not appealing to me anymore, if it ever had. I needed my own place and would begin a search tomorrow.

I lay awake with all that had happened rolling around in my head like a looped tape. After a sleeping pill, I went into a restless sleep, waking before my alarm. I felt horrible from all the emotional trauma from the last few days and my restless night. I got up, made coffee, and stared out the window into space. I hated lying, but called my office at eight, when I knew the phones would be on, and told my secretary that I had a family emergency and needed to be out of town for at least a week. After the usual expressions of sympathy, we figured out who could take my caseload and appointments, and I was free for the week.

My call to the office had consumed over an hour. I called Karen. They were already outside of the city, heading toward Interstate 80 and Iowa City. I could rent a car and meet them there. *Screw it. Why not? A week on the road. It might do me good, clear my head.*

I called a rental agency and they would pick me up in two hours, the time it would take to pack what clothes I thought I would need: some casual clothes I had, which wasn't much, underwear, toiletries, and I was ready to go. The rental car arrived and I dropped the agent's assistant back at his office and headed out of town. I cranked some tunes on the radio. Every mile from Chicago, I felt lighter, freer, more adventurous . . . and scared to death.

CHAPTER 13

I met up with the group at Russell and Karens' parents' farm near Iowa City that afternoon. I was nervous about seeing my ex-in-laws, but they were more than gracious toward me, making me feel more than welcome. So much had changed in the last few years since the divorce.

I had neither heard from Jess nor called her. When she left, our relationship seemed to be falling apart. I needed, I wanted to talk to her. I wanted to try to sort things out. So late the first night at the farm, I excused myself and went outside into a little garden area with several outdoor chairs and called. It would be early morning in Rome and I might catch her. Her cell went to voice mail. She had told me many times, before each and every trip she took, to always call her cell, never her hotel. That never did make any sense to me, so I decided to call her hotel and was quickly connected to her room. A man answered after the first ring.

"Bonjour, c'est Rémy."

"Oh, I'm sorry. They must have connected me to

the wrong room. I was calling for Jess . . ."

"Oh, Jessica. Of course. One moment. Jessica, sweetheart. You have a phone call, my love."

A moment later she answered. "Ciao, Marco? We should be there around ten thirty."

"This isn't Marco, and who the hell is Rémy, and what's with the 'sweetheart' and my love' stuff? What's going on?"

"Goddammit! I told you to never call my hotel! I can't talk now! Don't call back!" Before she could click off, I heard a child's voice. "Maman, qui est-ce?"

I stood there, staring off into the night with the phone still to my ear, waiting for someone to tell me it was a wrong number, that it hadn't been Jess, that it was somebody else named Jess. I felt dizzy, like I was suddenly transported into another dimension where nothing made sense. *Rémy? Sweetheart? My Love? Maman?* I felt nausea rising and I went to a bench and sat. I was barely able to breathe.

After a few minutes with my head between my knees, the nausea and dizziness passed. I called her cell. It went straight to voice mail. What would I say anyway? Nothing made sense. I had been in a relationship with this woman for over three years. She had a child? A family in Europe? Was she married? I suddenly felt like the biggest fool in the world. Several six-week-long trips to Europe every year interspersed with numerous week-long trips to New York. She wasn't just print-shopping. She was seeing her family. *What had I gotten myself into?*

Karen came and joined me. "Hey, you've been out here a long time. Are you okay? My god, you look like you've seen a ghost. What's wrong?"

My shock had turned to anger and now, with Karen, it turned to tears. I blathered out everything to her through my sobs.

"I'm such a fucking fool. How could I have been so blind and stupid? I don't know what to do."

Karen put her arm around me. "It will be okay. Truly. This is bullshit, but you're gonna be all right. You're with friends, whether you believe it or not."

We sat for a long time, not speaking. Karen's arm around me was comforting and felt good. Things were rolling through my mind like a runaway freight train. I didn't ever want to go back to Chicago, much less ever see Jess again. My life as I had known it was no more.

The next night I went in to help Karen with the merch table. It was exciting and took my mind off Jess. My anger with her had turned into seething hate. Neither Karen nor I had shared what had happened with the others. I tried to act normal, and must have, since no one seemed to notice my mood.

The next morning, Jess called. Her first words

were "What does 'Never call my hotel' mean to you, you stupid bitch? You could have ruined everything. Goddammit! Where are you?"

So I'm a bitch now? Interesting. I kept my cool, answering calmly, "I'm in Iowa, at Russell and Karen's parents' farm. I plan on hanging out with them for a week on the road, or maybe longer, if I feel like it."

"So what prompted that?" she asked, incredulous and angry.

"They invited me. Since you're off in Europe, I accepted their invitation and took a week off to travel with them. I needed a break, like you told me," I said with dripping sarcasm.

"Just like that? How can you just up and leave your work on the spur of the moment?"

"I lied and told them I had a family emergency," I answered with a chuckle.

"Dana, how could you be that stupid? If they ever find out you'll . . ."

I was smiling inwardly at her pathetic attempt to avoid the elephant lurking somewhere in the nether world of transatlantic cell phone connections.

"So what the fuck if they do. Right now, I don't give a shit, Jess-i-ca, my l-o-v-e!" I drawled with an exaggerated French accent. "So who the fuck is Rémy? And maman? You have a child?"

"He's a friend, just a friend. Nothing more.

And—"

"Yeah, right, my love. Sweetheart. Fuck you Jess. What are you? A fucking lesbian in Chicago and a hetero with a family in Europe? Fuck you!"

"You're overreacting. Really. You don't understand. There is an explanation."

"Overreacting? Explanation? You're the one with Rémy calling you 'sweetheart' and 'my love.' And who is calling you 'maman,' a trained monkey?" I asked with more sarcasm oozing from my words. "What the fuck is Rémy? A lesbian with a deep voice and a man's name?"

"I can explain . . ."

"I'm sure you can conjure up more lies, like all the lies of the last three years. Fuck you! I hope to god I never see you again. You're dead to me . . . Bitch!"

I clicked off and turned off my phone.

CHAPTER 14

The band played two nights in Iowa City, then onto Des Moines for two nights. I contacted my parents and asked if I could come and see them. My mother said it would be best if I didn't, since my father still had not gotten over my divorce and subsequent three-year relationship with a woman. I was both disappointed and a little relieved. I did manage to convince my mother to meet me for lunch. She was stiff and uncomfortable, which made me feel the same. We parted on awkward terms, promising to keep in touch.

After their gigs in Des Moines, we moved on to Omaha, Lincoln, Denver, Albuquerque, Santa Fe, and then Durango, Colorado. I called my office and extended my leave. I had settled into the rhythm of the road and was having the time of my life. My four companions were good to be with. They all now knew of my situation. However, my two weeks of freedom sadly came to an end and I had to get back. After tearful goodbyes, I flew out of Durango to Denver, then Chicago.

Back in Chicago, I reluctantly went from the airport to the condo. When I walked in, I got sick to my stomach. Thankfully, my stomach was empty and all I did was retch into the commode. I felt like a stupid fool, used by that two-timing, deceitful woman. I couldn't bear to stay there and went to a hotel. The next day I went into my office and resigned. I committed to two weeks to get my caseloads and affairs in order, and then I was free without a clue as to what I would do or where I would go. I knew Chicago was history.

CHAPTER 15

One year later

I walked out of my rented old adobe house, my home for the last nine months, two blocks off the plaza, into the dazzling, bright New Mexico morning sunlight. I put on my sunglasses. I'd learned early on to always have them with me. I loved living here in this amazing, magical place. The sky was bluer than any I could ever remember seeing. The desert and mountains offered spectacularly colorful canyons and vistas. Sunsets were most always as spectacular as Fourth of July fireworks.

During my trip with the Movers, I couldn't stop thinking of Santa Fe. The two nights and one day when I was there with them had been enough. I was smitten. During my two weeks finishing up at the Chicago office, I had made inquiries into some firms down there. Several were impressed by my resume, and one in particular sounded like a good fit. I flew to Albuquerque and took the commuter train up to Santa Fe for an interview with a man, not much older than me, who had started the firm and two others, a man and a woman, both closer to my age, a paralegal and an office manager.

The interview went well. All of us seemed to fit together well. I left the interview already thinking of these people as old friends. After passing the New Mexico bar exam, I was in full swing. I loved the work. Everyone was laid-back, normal workday dress being jeans and open-collar shirts, comfortable dresses, and slacks, unless we were in court—then it went more businesslike. We had a mixed group of clients. I was usually assigned to family and divorce cases, which were my expertise and my first love.

I had nobody in my life other than my colleagues, all now close friends. I kept in touch with Russell, Hannah, and Karen. It was like I'd been reborn. Everything was new and exciting. Santa Fe had so much to offer in culture, restaurants, and beautiful places to explore.

I had not heard anything from Jess since I left a little over a year ago. Then one day, to my surprise, I received a letter from her, with a Paris postmark. It had been sent to my parents in Des Moines and apparently my mother had forwarded it. My father would have most likely burned it. I left it unopened, sitting on my desk staring at me for over a week. Over lunch on a Friday, I told my female colleague, Susan, about it. She was the only one in the firm who knew anything much about my past, which I'd spilled out one night over dinner and too much wine.

Susanne insisted, "When we get back to the office, open it. At least, I want to know what she might have to say."

"You're just so incredibly nosy! All right, I'll do it, but I may need a drink afterward," I responded, chuckling as we walked back the single block to the office.

I sat down at my desk with Susanne sitting across from me, took a breath, cut it open and pulled out the single handwritten sheet of paper.

My dearest Dana,
I have finally gotten the nerve to write this. I want you to know that I was truly in love with you. I wanted to tell you about Rémy and little Isabella many times, but lacked the courage. I am ashamed of the way all this happened. I can only ask that you forgive me for my deceit, for which I am truly sorry.
I have sold my business in Chicago and moved permanently to Paris to be with my husband and child. He is an important and respected financier, and my absence was becoming a problem for him. I do love him and my daughter very much and am happy I made the decision to leave Chicago and my Midwest roots for good.

I am working for a gallery here in Paris, in Montmartre, that specializes in rare prints, so I am fortunate to be in my element. It's not the same as running my own business, but in many ways it is so much easier and less stressful. My French improves every day now. I am working on getting rid of my Chicago accent.

I think of you often and wonder where you are, how you are, if you are okay. I pray you are doing well. If you can find it in your heart, I would love to hear from you. Please forgive me.

With love and regret,
Jessica

I kept staring it for a moment, finally letting it slip from my hands onto my desk. So many memories flooded my head. My years of essentially surviving in Chicago. I was so naive and vulnerable those few years ago. *Never again.*

"Are you okay?" Susanne asked, interrupting my thoughts.

"I don't know. I feel like such a fool. This letter . . . This letter is just her bullshit, wanting forgiveness, wanting . . . wanting—'Love and regret?' What does that mean? I have no idea. I'm so done with her . . . Forever!" I was starting to choke up with anger, sadness, and regret.

241

"It's okay," Susanne said, trying weakly to reassure me. "It's okay. You're here. This is now. You've moved on and are continuing to move on. You have friends here. Good friends."

"I know, I know. I hear you. It's just . . . just hard."

"I can only imagine all you have told me. It's weird for me to comprehend, I know. I don't know what else to say."

"Say nothing. I know. Everything you say is true. It'll be okay. I was getting over all this and then she had to write this bullshit."

"It is bullshit. Total bullshit. So let it go."

"Thanks. Let's go out and have dinner and celebrate tonight. Celebrate freedom. Yeah!"

"It's a date. Let's do some lawyer shit. Okay?"

"Hell yeah. Let's do some law."

Finis

A Note from
the Author

If you enjoyed this book, I would be very grateful if you could write a review and publish it at your point of purchase. Your review, even a brief one, will help other readers to decide whether they'll enjoy my work.

Visit my website at www.elehner.com.

If you want to be notified of new releases from myself and other AIA Publishing authors, please sign up to the AIA Publishing email list at www.aiapublishing. com. Of course, your information will never be shared, and the publisher won't inundate you with emails, just let you know of new releases.

About the Author

Ed Lehner is a retired professor of graphic design from Iowa State University, a luthier, and musician. He has published two novels, *San Juan Sunrise* and *The Awakening of Russell Henderson*. He lived most of his life in Iowa and now resides in the Four Corners area of Colorado with his wife, Julie, and Emma the cat.